Changing Emma

John Brindley lives with his partner in the southeast of England. He has two children, both of whom have been instrumental in the development of his early stories for young people. John is a keen music fan and enjoys playing squash and socialising in London.

PETERS

FRASER

&

DUNLOP

500/4 THE CHAMBERS
CHELSEA HARBOUR
LONDON SW10 0XF

Also by John Brindley

Rhino Boy
The Terrible Quin
Turning to Stone

Changing Emma

John Brindley

Dolphin Paperbacks

First published in Great Britain in 2002
as a Dolphin Paperback
by Orion Children's Books
a division of the Orion Publishing Group Ltd
Orion House
5 Upper St Martin's Lane
London WC2H 9EA

A catalogue record for this book is available
from the British Library.

Typeset at The Spartan Press Ltd,
Lymington, Hants

Printed in Great Britain by
The Guernsey Press Co. Ltd, Guernsey, C.I.

ISBN 1 84255 201 5

One

The day Emma Green's GCSE results came through was the day her parents won twenty-three and a half million pounds on the National Lottery.

The results were good. Very good. A* in English, maths and physics, A in religious studies, geography, and art and design. B in French. French being her least favourite subject. Very, very good results.

Mr and Mrs Green were jumping up and down. 'We're off to sunny Spain,' they were singing, delighted. 'Say Ve-va Es-pania!'

'What's that?' Emma's old grandmother was saying from her chair, 'what's that?'

'We've won, Mum!' Emma's father bellowed at her, red in the face. 'We've only gone and won the lottery!'

'What have we won?' her grandmother said.

'Twenty-three million,' Mrs Green said.

'Twenty-three and a half, Vi,' Mr Green said. 'Don't forget the other five hundred thousand pounds. Don't forget that.'

Emma's mum, Violet, was shaking her head. 'Five hundred thousand pounds, and I forgot we even own it. See how quickly I've grown accustomed to being filthy, stinking, rotten rich?'

'Yeah!' Eddie shouted. 'Yeah! Filthy! Stinking! Rotten! Rich!' He threw his arms round his wife. They were jumping up and down together, po-going round the living-room.

Emma stood smiling, clutching her results letter. She watched Eddie and Vi in a pogo-clinch, Eddie's quiffed hair bouncing, Vi's glasses falling from her face. 'Come over here

3

Em,' Eddie's mother called to her only grandchild. 'Come over here,' she said, reaching out.

But the lottery winners were off-to-sunny-Spain again, living it up in the living-room, filthy rotten rich. 'Do you know what this means?' Eddie stopped suddenly to say to his mother and his wife.

Eddie's wife, Violet Green, a woman of one too many colours, retrieved her glasses and her breath. She was all steamed up, a dripping mess of adrenalin, sweat, saliva and tears. 'I don't know,' she gasped, 'I don't, really.' She burst into tears. Eddie laughed. He held her to his chest. Vi had to lean over his belly to get to his chest. But over she leaned, sniffing, laughing, crying and hiccoughing.

'Come here, Em,' Emma's grandmother said, taking her by the hand which was not holding the GCSE results letter.

'Do you know what this means?' Eddie said again.

'It means Emma's done really well,' her gran said.

'Yeah,' Eddie said, 'it does. But it also means that if we spent three and a half million quid straightaway, then invested the rest at, let's say, five per cent –'

Emma could feel her grandmother's surprisingly strong fingers holding her by the wrist.

'Five per cent,' her father went on, looking up at the ceiling, 'five per cent a year of twenty million gives you – gives you – what does that give you, Em? Can you work it out? How did your maths results go?'

'A*,' Emma said. She felt her grandmother's fingers tighten round her wrist as she said it.

'What's five per cent a year of twenty million quid?' her father said.

'A million,' Emma said.

'What? A million? A million pounds? – Did you hear that Vi, a million a year! We're going to be making it faster than we can spend it.'

Vi was nodding into his chest, overwhelmed with emotion.

4

'This is,' she was saying, or rather trying to say, 'this is – just – the most – it's the most –'

'I know Vi,' Eddie said. 'A million a year! Let's go out. Come on, let's go out.'

'No,' Violet looked up and said. 'Look at my face. What a state. I can't go out like this.'

'I'll go and get some champers,' Eddie said. 'Got any money?'

'I've got twenty-three and a half million,' Violet said, grinning through a face full of smeared mascara.

Emma tried to tell Helen, she really did. The day after the lottery win, Emma met her friend, her best friend, in the Italian café.

'I got six A's and a B,' Emma told Helen. 'How did you do?'

'Great. All A's. I was so excited, opening the letter and everything, weren't you?'

'Yes,' said Emma.

'My mum and dad were over the moon. They were like a couple of little kids.'

'So were mine,' Emma said, with the image of Vi and Eddie springing like young antelope all over the living-room. She had never seen her mother drunk, until last night. Vi had been crying with confused happiness as Eddie was smashing her champagne glass into the gas fire.

Eddie had been quaffing champagne out of a pint mug, smoking a big fat heavy cigar . . .

o o o

'You shouldn't smoke,' his mother, old Mrs Green, kept telling him. 'You know you shouldn't smoke. The house'll stink of it.'

'What difference does it make, now?' Eddie said. 'I've been a multimillionaire for, what, three days now. Three days without knowing it. I've got some catching up to do.'

'You still shouldn't smoke,' his mother told him, 'you know you shouldn't.'

'Lucky I checked those tickets,' Violet was saying, swaying, champagne spilling on to their best living-room carpet from another soon-to-be-broken glass.

6

'It doesn't matter now,' Eddie said, purposely spilling much more from his beer mug. 'Carpet like that. It doesn't matter now.'

Last night, Emma had watched her father pouring expensive bubbles into the carpet of their living-room, then smashing his big glass against the bars of the gas fire. Violet had staggered back, laughing, falling against the dining-table.

'Look out!' Eddie was laughing. 'Vi's legless. Here, Mum, try some of this champagne, come on. And you, Em. Come on, let's celebrate.' He poured them both a small glass.

'I don't want it,' Emma said.

'She don't want it,' her grandmother said.

'I know!' cried Eddie. 'A toast! A toast!'

'A toast!' Vi echoed, holding up a new glass.

Emma's grandmother grabbed up an empty glass. 'To Emma's whopping results,' she said. Vi and Eddie both stared at her in surprise.

o o o

'My mum and dad were over the moon,' Helen said to Emma the next day as they were sitting in the Italian café in town. 'They were like a couple of little kids.'

Emma remembered Vi and Eddie jumping round the room together. 'So were mine,' she said.

'We had champagne,' Helen said.

'So did we,' Emma said. So did the carpet, and the fireplace, and Eddie's shirt, she was thinking. Her mind was running this way and that, trying to decide just how she should be feeling about any of this.

'It's horrible, isn't it?' Helen said.

Sitting with Helen in the Italian café, thinking of Eddie's confused face as her grandmother had proposed the toast to the GCSE results, Emma couldn't quite decide what, or how, to think.

'It's horrible, isn't it?' Helen was saying.

'What is?' Emma asked, picturing the champagne dripping from her father's chin.

'Champagne,' Helen said. 'It's *horrible*, isn't it?'

'Yes,' Emma said. 'My dad says that nobody likes the stuff, not really. But he says you have to have it when you've got something really worth celebrating.'

'My mum and dad like it,' Helen said. 'They say it's a mature flavour. They say you'll like it when you grow up.'

Emma was thinking of Eddie and Vi tipping champagne from the bottle over each other's head. 'I expect they're right,' she said.

'Anyway,' Helen said, 'my mum and dad are going to let me have some champagne at the party on Saturday, because we've all got something really worth celebrating, haven't we?'

'Yes,' Emma said, enthusiastically.

Helen, sensing her friend's altered emphasis, said, 'What's the matter?'

'Oh, nothing. You know – nothing, really.'

'Nothing really? What's the matter?'

'Oh – it's just that –'

But the glass door to the café flew open at that moment. Helen looked past Emma. 'Oh no!' she said.

o o o

Emma had tried to tell Helen that day in the Italian café. But it wasn't easy. The exam results were everything they had talked about, had concentrated on for months and months. That was what the party was going to be for, to celebrate. Helen's parents were going to have champagne.

Emma tried to tell her about the money. But, as Eddie Green had said, time and again, 'Everything's changed.'

So it was difficult to let Helen know that exam results no longer seemed to matter so much. What was the point? Violet and Eddie Green had lived in hope that their daughter would do well, that she would be successful. Then, suddenly, unexpectedly, success beyond their wildest, most insane dreams just flopped into their laps.

Everything had changed.

Emma found that she couldn't any longer share Helen's sense of importance. Trying for good grades, working your way through subjects with no practical use – it all seemed suddenly so, so irrelevant.

Who was going to need a job in an office somewhere, or teaching stupid kids in a graffiti secondary school for the rest of their lives?

'The world,' Eddie had said to his daughter, 'is your heavily pearled oyster my dear. Everything you ever wanted is here, already, done and dusted.'

Violet had been weeping. She was tipsy on champagne, stumbling to find words to express her overcharged emotions. 'I've always felt,' she was trying to say to Eddie's mother, old Mrs Green, 'I've always felt, you know –'

'That's right,' Eddie was chipping in. 'Better, that's how I've always felt.'

'Yes,' Violet said, 'better. That's it. Better than her and him at number sixteen. Better than all of them next door.'

'Yeah!' roared Eddie. 'We don't care what car they've got now, Vi. We're better than that, whatever it is!'

That was the beginning. Violet, mascara-smeared and tiddly, with Eddie pouring sparkling wine into what had been their best carpet, had always felt something different, something better.

'The world is ours,' Eddie had said, in the beginning, before the world really did show them what money was made of.

That day, sitting in the Italian café with Helen, Emma had struggled to find what to say. She suddenly felt like laughing in her friend's face.

Helen, sensing something strange about her, had said, 'What's the matter?'

'Oh, nothing, You know – nothing, really.'

'Nothing really? What's the matter?'

'Oh – it's just that –'

That's when Claire Thomas had entered the Italian café with Dan 'Fidget' Godman. From then on, it was the usual. Helen hated Claire, Claire Helen. From then on it was listening to Helen slanging Claire, the two of them doing daggers at each other across the tiled floor of the café.

'She only goes around with him', Helen started to say to Emma, 'for one thing. He's Robbie Britto's mate, and he's got a car.'

'That's two things,' Emma said.

'I don't care,' Helen said, 'she's a user, that's all I do know. She uses Fidget to get to Rob. She's a user. She's used me, she uses everyone. I hate her.'

Emma sat back and listened. It all seemed so small-minded, so paltry and insignificant. If she wanted to, Emma could walk out of the café this very minute and go and get a brand-new car of her own. And someone to drive it. She could buy anything she liked. There wasn't anything for sale in this whole town that Emma couldn't afford.

It was such a wonderful feeling. It put her comfortably, amusingly, outside all the bickering and the character clashes that went on causing so much trouble. The situation between the ex-best friends, Helen and Claire, was a long-standing feud with so many causes and concerns that Emma had long ago stopped trying to keep up with it all. In truth, she had always been slightly afraid of Claire. She was surprised how Helen, who'd usually go out of her way to avoid a row, would argue so recklessly with her.

So Emma didn't tell her anything. She simply sat back, for once in her life enjoying the needle bickering by being so removed from it. She felt removed from everything as she watched Helen glancing past her towards Claire and Fidget while they waited for Robbie Britto.

Robbie's father owned the Italian café. He was standing

behind the counter, also glancing over at Claire and especially at Fidget Godman. Mr Britto looked on distastefully as Fidget bobbed and bounced in his seat, his fingers clicking and snapping. Emma could see them all. Helen in front of her, Claire and Fidget just behind to Emma's left, Robbie's dad behind the counter.

Look at them all. Look at their petty dislikes, their strained expressions. The little things that mattered to them were to Emma as tiny nothings on the face of the earth. This was all so little to get excited about. All so very insignificant. The whole world was waiting for Emma just outside the glass doors of Mr Britto's Italian café. What was there here to concern her any longer? Why should she care? She didn't care.

Then, that day in the café, the full force of not having to care elevated her into a kind of dumb euphoria. She said nothing, but looked out and down at the tiny pinpoint of her previous focus and found it entirely lacking. She found it all an absurd joke.

'The rocket scientists are in again,' she heard Claire say to Fidget.

Helen turned on her. 'Did you get your results, Claire?' she said. 'Did you pass your home economics? I hope so. You're going to need it.'

'Oh, I did all right, thanks. How about you? You'll be doing your trainspotter's A-level next I expect?'

They were glaring at each other. Emma sat in what would usually be a very uncomfortable situation without a care. Let them bicker. Let Mr Britto stare at Fidget's nervous tics, his bobbing legs, his drumming, snapping fingers. Let Robbie Britto appear at the door thinking that everyone fancied him.

Emma started to laugh. She didn't care.

'What was so funny?' Helen said, outside. 'Come on, what are you laughing at? Are you completely mad?'

'I must be,' Emma said, starting to cough through her laughter. 'I think I am, completely insane.'

'I think you are, too,' Helen said, straight-faced.

Emma was still coughing. 'But –' she was trying to say, 'not – as – not as – insane as all that lot –' she managed to say, indicating back up the road to the Italian café.

'I know,' Helen said. 'That cow! Did you hear what she said to me about us?'

Emma was nodding, almost speechless, practically choking with withheld laughter. She nodded, nodded.

'She's just a user,' Helen went on, back on to her favourite subject. 'How anybody can put up with her, I don't know. Did you know', she said, 'that she's still coming to the party on Saturday?'

'Is she?' Emma managed to say.

'My parents have only gone and invited her. I told her, to her face, I said I didn't want her there. But she just said, too bad, she said. She's just coming to wind me up, I know she is. If she spoils it for me –' Helen was saying, as they made their way up the road.

Emma had to start laughing again. She could hardly breathe. It was a joke, the whole thing. How could Helen take it all so seriously?

'What are you laughing at all the time?' Helen turned and said. 'What's the matter with you?'

Emma shrugged. She was snorting with laughter as Helen looked more and more irritated with her.

12

'I wish I knew what was so funny,' Helen said, starting off again, clearly irritated.

Emma tried to tell her, really she did. But it wouldn't come out. The timing was all wrong. Everything was too, too, too absurd for words.

Helen left her on the corner. 'Look, I'll see you at the party on Saturday, if I don't see you before. I've got a lot to do between now and then,' she said, stalking away.

Emma could have shouted at the sky with the intensity of her release. She was free, free of all the stuff and nonsense that made Helen so tight and so tense. Helen was so – so straight!

So Emma didn't say anything. She wanted to save it for the right time, which would be soon, but not yet. She would know the right moment, when it came. Oh yes, she would recognise her time. *Her time*. It was coming. It was very nearly here. But not yet. She had to stop herself from shouting out, from running and jumping all the way home.

Home? This place? It had changed so much, because she had. The carpets wanted more champagne, the fireplace more broken glasses. This was such a little place, for little people. The concerns and the preferences of the Italian café were rife here, written into the furniture and the fabric of the curtains. Emma looked around the place, feeling the difference. This place could not possibly contain her now, could not possibly give full expression to what she could and would become.

Her grandmother was sitting there in her old chair, seemingly the same as ever. There she was, with that little, paltry house and all their sorry belongings ranged around her in complacent and humble poor taste.

'Are you back?' she asked.

'Yes,' Emma said, but thinking that, in fact, she was not. Not in the way the old lady meant, anyway.

'Are you making a cup of tea?' her Nan asked. 'I haven't had one all morning. My legs are playing me up today, real bad.'

13

'I'll make you a cup of tea, Nan,' Emma said. 'Where's Mum and Dad?'

'Oh, I don't know. How would I know?'

Emma went to make the tea. The kitchen was like a foreign field, with small canisters labelled Tea and Coffee and Sugar that Emma had never bothered noticing before. The labels might have been written in another language, the clock ticking on the wall telling nothing but of a time before this.

'I need this,' Emma's grandmother said, sipping her tea.

'What time did Mum and Dad go out?' Emma said.

Her Nan didn't know. She shook her head. 'They were gone early,' she said. 'Eddie's going for cars. And houses.'

Emma smiled. It sounded so strange. And yet it was true. They were out shopping. For cars and houses. 'It's good, isn't it?' Emma smiled. 'They can afford anything they like. Absolutely anything.'

Her grandmother snorted. 'Good, is it?'

'Course it is, Nan. It's everything.'

Emma felt herself being looked at, long and hard. 'Everything, is it? Is that right?'

'Course it is, Nan. Don't be such a wet blanket. We've made it. This is it.'

'Oh,' her Nan said. 'And I thought this,' she said, looking round at the old living-room, 'was it.'

'Oh, Nan,' Emma said, 'come on. Things change. If they change for the better, then everything's all right, isn't it?'

'Yes. If they change for the better.'

'Then everything's all right, isn't it? Everything's better. Isn't it?'

Everything was better. Paris was like a dream of heaven.

In truth, any big city would have done for Emma and her father to be wealthy in. But Paris it was and wealthy were they. Filthy. Stinking. Rotten.

Emma's mother couldn't make it. Emma's grandmother wasn't very well, so somebody had to stay home and look after her. The old lady wouldn't allow, she kept insisting, some stranger or the other to come into her home to 'do' for her. She didn't like those people, she said, as if she already knew them all.

Old Mrs Green was Eddie's mother, which might have meant that he and not she should have to stay behind. Eddie, however, wasn't very good at tending the sick. Vi couldn't trust him to feed Nan, she said, let alone be sure to give her the right tablets at the right time.

For Emma, secretly, it could not have worked out any better. Eddie was a rich man. He lived it immediately, with an immediacy that kind of money deserved. Emma wouldn't have wanted to go with her mother alone. It would have been a French Marks and Sparks, duty-frees then home on the early ferry.

As it turned out, it was perfect. They were first-class passengers into the heart of designer fashion and the kind of champagne glitz reserved for disposable incomes of well over half a million filthy stinking pounds a year.

Emma lost her mind. That is, an outlook far broader replaced the mind she'd grown into for sixteen years, with a money perspective that vindicated her mockery of the Green family's little workaday lives so far.

'Who would've imagined it,' Eddie Green was forever sitting back saying, as he surveyed one sumptuous luxury after another.

'Go for it, girl,' he'd say to Emma in response to her bristle of fear at the sheer magnitude of the prices written in green ink on the labels of all the clothes, but easily translated into mega-bucks sterling. Eddie Green laughingly paid seven hundred pounds for a single dress for his daughter.

Emma was thrilled speechless. She'd have to tell someone, everyone. At the party on Saturday, she'd just have to tell everyone that she was wearing seven hundred pounds worth of dress alone.

How much for those shoes? How can any pair of shoes be worth that much?

'Go for it, girl,' Eddie said. 'You're going to the party in style. The night belongs to you, don't forget it. You are it. Numero Uno. My daughter.' He smiled as he accepted another coffee from the shop assistant, for which he would fork out six pounds fifty a throw.

'I can earn more than that in the time it takes to drink it,' Eddie said, which thought warmed them into the purchase of a jacket for Emma it would once have taken Eddie two months wages to pay for.

'Helen's parents like champagne,' Emma told Eddie as he sipped from a long fluted glass over a lobster lunch, 'can I take them some on Saturday?'

He nodded. 'Of course you can. A crate?' he said.

Emma stalled. She'd only meant a single bottle of something ultra-expensive.

'Two,' Eddie said, quickly. 'Two crates then. Yes. That's my girl. Go get 'em. You're going in style. Nothing but the best for my little girl.'

o o o

Emma was going in style. She felt nervous, a little self-conscious turning up at the party wearing the obvious expense of Paris designer fashion, wearing make-up, completed by the ultimate accessory of two boxes of twelve bottles of bubbly.

But the effect was devastating. She blew them all away. Nobody even so much as bothered mentioning her exam results. Nor Helen's, after she broke the twenty-three and a half million pound news.

The night belonged to Emma Green. She intimidated all the other girls there. She danced like never before. She owned the place. Even Robbie Britto wanted to get to know her. Well, he couldn't. Not yet. Not just yet.

She didn't really know herself yet. She was brand-new, fresh out of the box, glistening and enviable. Everything was better. Even Robbie noticed her. The dream of heaven was about to come true.

Emma was looking forward to seeing Helen's response. She was glad she'd saved the news for tonight. 'You wait till Helen finds out,' Emma had said to her Nan as she'd been getting ready for the party.

But Emma's Nan just sat in her old chair moaning about not being able to understand the importance of it all. She was complaining about the changes. Old people were like that, they didn't like change. But they all had to move on. Things were different. They were moving into a new house. As easily as that. Cash transaction. Sign here, it's yours.

But Emma's old grandmother had to go on and on complaining about it. She didn't want to go anywhere, she said. She couldn't see why they had to move. They didn't have to. It wasn't compulsory. She'd lived in that house ever since she'd got married. Eddie had bought it from the council. She didn't want to go anywhere.

She didn't like being left on her own for the evening, but still wouldn't let them get anyone in. 'I'm not a baby,' she said. Emma left her on her own, sitting in her old chair.

o o o

The cab driver loaded Emma's champagne into the boot of his car. 'Wow,' he said, 'you're going for it tonight.'

'Yes,' she smiled. Yes, she was going for it tonight all right.

'Some party then,' her driver said as they pulled away from the old house. 'Who's going to be there? Anyone I've heard of?'

'Yes,' Emma said. 'Me.'

The taxi driver looked into his mirror at her.

I'll be there, Emma was thinking, looking back at him. Me. Emma Green. The new, bold Emma Green; the one that never, ever looks back.

And if you haven't heard of Emma Green yet, don't worry; you will.

o o o

Emma Green and Robbie Britto.

Robbie Britto actually breezed over at the party and said to Emma, 'You're a good dancer,' he said. Just like that. As if he meant it.

Emma knew she wasn't, but it was really something to hear him say she was. It made her feel good about herself, as if she could have been a good dancer with just a little more encouragement from him. The others hated her for it. Claire Thomas especially. Emma could see Claire staring at her the whole night. Emma loved it. It felt so powerful, so exciting.

Suddenly the evening had changed. This was no longer Helen's little party to celebrate a few school exam results. This was now Emma's night, the lottery winners' daughter looking and feeling better than she'd ever looked or felt in her whole life.

Robbie Britto was looking at her while she danced. He was coming over to talk to her. Everyone was talking about her. They were all watching her. She was the one in the centre of the collected attention, the one winning Rob's special attention.

Helen, she noticed, stayed away. She seemed intimidated by her friend's newfound confidence. In many ways, that felt right too. Things were beginning to change for Emma.

She'd been to Paris for the day to buy clothes. Her father said they could go on Concorde soon to New York, to buy clothes. Her parents were going to buy a new house. Brand new, with a massive garden, big drive, and a swimming pool. A swimming pool! They couldn't even swim, Emma's mum and dad. The pool was for her. A swimming pool, just for her.

She was feeling fantastic. Robbie Britto was interested in the lottery winners' daughter. Of course he was. She didn't blame him for that. If she didn't have parents that were multimillionaires all of a sudden, he wouldn't have ever noticed her.

But that was because she had been unnoticeable. Like Helen. Helen was wearing a neat little frock for the party, with her hair tied up. She looked like a too-young schoolteacher. That's what Emma had looked like. That's how they'd both behaved, as if getting good grades was the most important thing in the world.

Maybe it was for Helen. But it wasn't for Emma. Not any more. There were more important things in life.

Life! Yes, that's what she wanted now. Some life. She wanted excitement all of a sudden. She knew she wanted it as soon as she got a taste for it at the party with Robbie Britto looking at her and Claire giving her absolute daggers from the other side of the room. It was wonderful to be the centre of attention for a change, to be wearing clothes nobody else could afford, to be dancing and not caring what people thought.

19

Rob thought she looked all right. He said so. He said she looked wild. Well, pretty wild is what he actually said. Which, for Emma, at that time, was wild indeed.

She laughed more that evening than she had the whole of the rest of her life. Helen kept out of her way. She had said hello when Emma first arrived, but in a strange way. She was surprised by Emma's appearance, of course. The new clothes. The hair and make-up. Quite a change. Emma had felt a little self-conscious, turning up with two whole crates of very expensive champagne for Helen's parents. That feeling didn't last long.

Helen had looked at her strangely. Helen's parents were more than a little surprised by all the champagne. Then she told them about the twenty-three and a half million pound lottery win.

Everything changed.

She danced as if she'd never danced before in her life. Which, in fact, she hadn't. Not really. Not like this. She was dancing as if she didn't care. Which she didn't. She was attracting more attention and admiration than ever. And more hostility. Especially from Claire, when Robbie started looking at her. Especially when Robbie came over to tell her she looked pretty wild.

Emma was smiling at him. She didn't stop dancing, even then. She couldn't. She felt too good. She felt pretty wild.

Rob was soon dancing with her. Claire, who was supposed to be there with Rob and Fidget, was determined not to look at them. But Emma could see she couldn't help it. She'd only come in the first place to wind Helen up, but was getting wound up herself, big time. Emma could see it in her face. The jealousy. She'd never made anyone jealous before.

She liked it. A lot. An awful lot.

o o o

Rob encouraged her. She felt encouraged by his attention. He told her she was different. He didn't know why he hadn't noticed it before.

Emma danced all night at the party. She hardly spoke to anyone at all, except Robbie. They were talking, laughing and joking together all evening. Claire was trying to dance with Fidget, who was like an electric stick-man. Claire was livid, everyone could see.

Rob and Emma laughed and laughed. Helen didn't. You'd have thought she would, but she didn't.

'I can't think why I never noticed you until now,' Rob kept saying to Emma.

'I can think of twenty-three and a half million reasons,' Emma laughed.

'Fair point,' Rob said, laughing too.

Emma suffered from no illusions. She enjoyed the attention. She really, really liked Rob, but if the lottery win hadn't happened, then none of this would. But she was glad it was happening. She was better at it than she could ever have dreamed. She was as witty as Robbie Britto. She wasn't such a bad dancer, at least as good as all the other girls. Better than Helen. Much better than that. Maybe not as good as Claire, but Claire had to dance with Fidget, so it didn't count. Besides, Emma just looked so much better than all the others. The clothes she wore did so much for her. She was going to change her image, beginning right now. She was going to be so much more like the sort of girl Robbie Britto would be attracted to over girls like Claire Thomas.

Emma invited Rob to come and see her new house, as soon after they moved in as he liked. 'It's going to have a pool and everything,' she told him.

'A pool?'

'Swimming pool. You should see the size of it.'

'I'd like to,' he said. 'When? Tell me when, so I can get some time off work.'

Emma could hardly breathe, she felt so excited. The music had stopped by this time, the party was winding down. But Emma was still up, wound up and excited by Rob's response to her invitation. She watched him as he went to get his jacket from the bedroom.

Helen sidled over as soon as she saw Rob go out. She and Emma had hardly shared two words together the whole evening. 'You've been having a good time,' Helen said.

Emma had to laugh. 'Well, wouldn't you?' she said.

Helen was looking very serious with her. 'You look different,' she said.

Emma laughed again. 'Well, wouldn't you?' she said again, glancing through the doorway to the hall.

Helen was fidgeting beside her. 'Yes,' she was saying, 'I suppose I would. You went to Paris, didn't you?'

'Yes,' Emma said. She was being distracted by what she could see in the hall.

'Yes,' Helen was saying, 'Claire had to tell me. She asked me why I didn't know.'

The door was half open. Through it, at the bottom of the stairs, Emma could see Rob talking to Claire.

'When did you find out?' Helen was asking.

Emma was watching Rob smiling into Claire's face.

'Why didn't you tell me?' Helen said. 'You must have known for ages.'

'What?' Emma said. Helen was standing in her way. 'What?'

'About the money: why didn't you tell me?'

'I wanted to – to surprise you.'

'Yes,' Helen said, as Emma watched Claire laughing at something Rob was saying, 'you surprised me all right. But I'd have thought –'

'Look,' Emma said suddenly, moving past her, 'I tell you

what, I'll call you. We can have a nice long chat about it, okay? I'll call you. We'll be moving soon.'

'Moving?' Helen said, almost calling out to her. 'You're moving?'

'Of course,' Emma said. She was standing by the door. She could hear the sound of Claire's over-conspicuous laughter.

'Why are you moving?'

'Why? Because – why do you think?'

'Where are you going?'

'Not far,' Emma said. 'I'll call you. You can come over. Bring your swimming stuff. We're going to have a pool.'

Emma left her. She knew Helen was standing there wanting more from her. But standing there in that dreadful party frock while Claire was laughing with Robbie just outside the door . . .

'How are you getting home, Rob?' Emma said, distracting Rob's attention from Claire's silly face smiling in front of him.

'I don't know,' Rob said.

'We've got a cab coming,' Claire said, glancing at Emma.

Emma stood firm in her new clothes and confidence. This didn't feel so bad. In fact, she could really start to enjoy this kind of competition, because she felt she could win.

'Why don't you walk with me?' she said, ignoring Claire's hostile glances. 'It's a really warm night.'

'Why not?' Rob shrugged. He smiled. Claire didn't. 'I'll just go and tell Fidge what we're doing,' he said.

Emma and Claire were left at the foot of the stairs, standing together in an ugly, aggressive silence. But Emma felt all right about it. She was glancing everywhere but at Claire, rocking slightly from side to side, sweetly enjoying the feel of Claire's rising animosity.

'You think you're it now,' she heard Claire saying, quietly, to her.

23

'I beg your pardon, Claire?' she said, looking sweetly back at her. 'Did you say something?'

'You know what I said,' Claire hissed. 'You heard me.'

Emma raised her eyebrows. 'I don't think I did, Claire. But – here's Fidget for you,' she said, as Fidge came from the kitchen with Rob just behind him.

'Cab's here,' Fidget clicked and skipped, passing straight through towards the front door.

'We're walking,' Rob called to him. 'See you tomorrow, probably.'

Fidget Godman waved a fluttering hand without turning round. He went out.

'Cab's there,' Rob said to Claire. Claire faltered. 'See you, then,' Rob said to her.

'Yes,' Emma said, 'see you then, *Claire*.'

∘ ∘ ∘

They walked through the dark evening towards Emma's home, with Rob telling Emma what it was like being a DJ.

'Fidget's my MC,' he was saying, 'I do the mixing.'

Emma pretended to understand what he was talking about. She had a vision of Rob going through the crowd laughing and joking with everybody.

'We've got a regular gig in town, in Mallory's on Friday nights. You should come down.'

'I'd love to,' Emma said. 'But only if you're coming to my pool party on Monday.'

'I'll see if I can get the afternoon off,' he said.

'Good.'

'Can I bring Fidge with me?'

'Of course you can,' Emma said, taking off her jacket. 'Why don't you let Fidge bring Claire, too?' she said, smiling.

It was a very warm night.

o o o

'Where've you been until this time?' her grandmother started saying to her as soon as Emma walked back into their old house that night.

This would be the last night she'd be walking back into this. Everything was boxed, most of it destined for the charity shop. Emma thought it should go straight to the dump, for what it was worth. Still, there was no telling what some people could make use of.

Her old grandmother sat unboxed as yet in her same-as-ever old chair. She started questioning Emma as soon as she came through the door as if nothing had changed.

'Where've you been until this time?' she said, as if Emma was still supposed to be answerable to her.

'I've been – having the time of my life,' Emma said. 'I've been –'

Her grandmother snorted. 'Time of your life? You haven't experienced any life yet.'

'No,' Emma said, 'but now I'm having some. Where's Mum and Dad?'

'Your mum's in bed. She's not too well now. That's no surprise either. What do they think they're doing, out all over the place all the time?'

'Enjoying themselves?'

'You think so? I don't think so.'

'Oh, Nan. Don't be such an old – don't be so stuffy,' Emma said, just about preventing herself from calling her Nan an old fart.

Emma was still flying, carried away on an adrenalin high. The old disapproving widow in her threadbare chair wanted only to bring everything down with her complaints and her regrets. What was there to regret? They were rich. They were stinking, rotten rich!

'Your dad might be enjoying himself,' Emma's Nan said, 'for all I know. You may be. Your mum's not.'

'She's all right,' Emma said. 'She can't wait to get away from here and into the new house. Neither can I.'

Her Nan snorted.

Emma didn't care, why should she? What was the point of hanging on to this place, to all this junk? There were better places to go, things to get. Look at that chair the old widow clung to for her life. Threadbare. Worn out.

Time for a clear-out. High time for a damned good clear-out.

Another crystal blue day the next morning. Everything looked pristine, glistening, perfect.

Everything, that is, except Emma's dad. He looked like a wreck. The police, local newspaper reporters, all sorts of people were turning up at the old house in the middle of the estate.

This morning, pristine blue and clear, they were saying goodbye to all this. Emma was up early, still buzzing, putting her few things together. She wasn't taking much. Her new clothes, some make-up. Nothing else.

This was a parting of the ways.

The neighbours were out there to watch them go. And the local press. The police had been round too. Actually, they had delivered Emma's father, scraping him off the floor of a police car.

He had staggered in early, red eyes blinking in the already hot sun. He was laughing with the young policemen, who were slapping him on the back, all the very best of friends.

Emma was just up, but there was her Nan, sitting everlastingly in her old patched chair by a cold gas fire. She was done up as if it was the middle of winter with a blizzard raging outside. She was red-eyed too, from sitting in her chair all night worrying about her son.

Emma could see by the look on her face that her bad boy was home again. She could see the old woman sitting up like this through winter nights long gone, waiting for her wayward only son to bring the wild night in with him for her disapproval.

'No harm done,' he was saying to the young policemen.

They were shaking their heads. 'No, none at all,' one of them said. 'I'd be doing the same if I was in your shoes.'

Emma watched her father shake them by the hand. They left him there. He turned to face her, blinking through puffy eyes. He smiled at Emma, shrugging. Emma was standing in the doorway of the living-room. She, smiling back, indicated with a slight nod of her head, to her grandmother sitting cold over the gas fire.

Her father pulled a face. He went to sneak off up the stairs with an exaggerated loping gait.

'Eddie,' his mother called out. Her voice rang as if the house was already empty. Emma laughed as her father, caught out, came plodding in like a shamefaced schoolboy. Her grandmother glared at her before saying, 'Vi's not very well, you know. You do know that, don't you?'

He glanced at Emma. She was trying not to laugh. There he stood, her father, having suffered years and years of tedious work, night after night in front of the telly with his home-brew beer and no money in his pockets. Of course he was out kicking up some dust. Who wouldn't be? He had all those years and years to make up for.

But he suffered his old mother's glare out of respect for his elders. There he stood, multimillionaire, richest and most powerful man in the whole dead drab town, rumbled like a naughty child before the stern countenance of his disapproving mother. Emma wanted to laugh. She didn't, somehow, but had to look out of the window as the old lady admonished her son for a fool old enough to know better. 'Old enough not to care,' Emma heard him say.

Yes, she thought, yes. She herself knew no better, so didn't care. He knew, but didn't care anyway. That's what made it right. They were above all this, the cold disapproval of the gas fire, the threadbare chair with all its years of making do, and tiresome, tedious effort.

'Come on, Nan,' Emma said, taking her father's arm, 'let us

off. We're only out for a bit of fun.' Emma looked at the love and amusement in her father's unshaven face.

'It's Violet I'm worried about,' old Mrs Green was saying, looking away from her son and granddaughter.

'What you worried about me for?' Violet Green said on entering the living-room in her dressing-gown. 'I'm all right. You don't need to go worrying about me.'

'There she is,' Eddie said, holding out his arms.

'What you been up to?' Violet said to him, eyeing his red-eyed, plump and stubbly face.

'No good,' said old Mrs Green.

Eddie was shrugging. 'Shenanigans,' he said. 'A little high jinks. Celebrating, innit?'

Emma's mum was laughing. Emma too. So was her dad. He was still hung-over, unwashed and smelling like fried-onion flavoured skunk. Only the old lady turned away, stuck by bad legs in her chair and by old age into a narrow, provincial way of thinking.

'We're moving today,' Violet smiled and said. 'We're on our way.'

'We're on our way,' Eddie repeated, hugging her.

'Here,' Eddie said, holding out a free arm to his daughter, 'Em, come over here.' Emma fell into the embrace. They were on their way. The three of them, on the threshold of a new life, with the old one left worn out in a worn-out, threadbare, grubby armchair.

o o o

They closed the front door for the last time. Eddie did it. Emma and her mother were standing in the garden, watching. Eddie's mother was in the hire-car, watching.

The neighbours were out. The press were there. *Heigh-Ho!* magazine had paid a small fortune to cover the day. Emma was having the money. Photographs of the old place, then the new. Before, after. What a contrast. *Heigh-Ho!* magazine!

Emma was so excited. They were going to be a feature spread. *Heigh-Ho!* magazine! Everyone she knew read it. And she was going to be the main feature in the next edition! Yes!

She thought of them all, everyone she knew, everyone she didn't know, all looking at her in the feature spread pages of *Heigh-Ho!* The mag was always full of celebs. That's what they were going to be. That's what they were becoming.

They were celebrities, up there with the best. There soon wouldn't be a film or pop star that wouldn't know about the Green family.

Everyone was astonished when Emma's father suddenly picked up a stone from the front garden and hurled it straight through one of the windows downstairs. He was laughing like a drunkard. He danced like a drunkard with his wife and daughter. The press were snapping away recording every event on still video cameras.

The press got him to do the stone-throwing stunt again as they'd all missed it the first time. So again he found another stone and smashed another window. Again he danced drunk and laughing with his wife. She, looking palely bemused, smiled for the cameras before climbing into the back of the hire-car beside Eddie's mother.

Emma was watching her. The neighbours were out in force. Her and him at number sixteen, all of them from next door out standing next to their cars – and Violet was disappointing Emma by creeping away quietly, looking fuzzily from the back of the car with old Mrs Green at the two smashed windows of her dear old home.

'What will you do with the old house now?' the *Heigh-Ho!* mag reporter was saying to Emma's father.

Emma was watching the way her dad was looking at the reporter. She was small, with a head of furious red hair and a red suit with a short skirt.

Emma's father smiled at the reporter before saying, 'We're

going to sell it of course. And Emma's going to have the money, aren't you Em?'

Emma's mother was still blinking at the two broken windows. Emma was stalking with her father in front of *Heigh-Ho!*'s glamorous reporter. The camera man was snapping up the centre feature images.

Old Mrs Green looked out with Violet from the back of the hire-car. Emma looked round and saw her face. She looked round and caught sight of the age-old disapproval in her expression.

What would *she* know? At her time of life, how could she know what it was going to be like being young and wealthy? Young, and wealthy, and beautiful. What would *she* know?

o o o

Heigh-Ho! magazine were there again next day. That was good. That was very, very good.

The lady reporter was back with notepad and digital recorder, a fluffy microphone and a droopy photographer by her side. She was dressed all in green today. Her wristwatch and glasses were green.

'Green for the Greens,' she said to Emma's father. Emma had watched them smile at each other.

Today was the day of the swimming-pool shots. It was still hot and sunny. A few early clouds had melted away under the fierce insistence of the sun. This was right. This was perfect for Emma, this early sunshine, the smiles her father lavished on Amanda, the green *Heigh-Ho!* interviewer.

In the house, Emma's mum was being snapped by the photographer as he sank cup after cup of coffee. Violet Green was keen to be shown against the backdrop of her new interest in art. She particularly enjoyed sculpture, she told the magazine, as she was being featured with her porcelain shire horses with little leather reins and old-fashioned plough complete with shirtsleeved ploughman.

31

This was perfect. The others would be arriving soon. Emma's pool party. The new house. The huge garden. This place was a mansion. It had pillars by the front doors and by the garage doors. Talk about class. They were moving up, in style.

Emma could see the flash of the photographer's camera going. They'd locked old Mrs Green in her room for the morning to stop her complaining to *Heigh-Ho!*

Besides, *Heigh-Ho!*'s readers wouldn't want to catch sight of the old girl's ragged old chair. No one would want to see her toothless mouth first thing in the morning. Especially on a morning like this. Emma wanted everything to be perfect. She had a pretty good idea what perfect meant, too.

When Amanda from *Heigh-Ho!* went into the house to interview Violet, Emma approached her father. He was reclining by the pool, afraid to go into the water, but extremely happy to languish on the sunny edge with orange juice and coffee, a small mountain of scrambled eggs and toast.

'This is more like it,' he said, as Emma came to sit near him.

She nodded. She was wearing her new swimsuit already, the one from Paris with the high, high legs and lowest of low backs.

'You look great,' he said. 'You really look the part, you know?' he said, nodding towards the house.

Emma looked at their new house. Her mother was filling it very quickly with every stick of antique furniture she could lay her hands on, some of it even older than four years. The ornamental farmyard implements, oil paintings of rural scenes and cute china labourers were proliferating throughout. The wall lights were each adorned with two corner cherubs, fat golden babies with wings.

But in amongst the clutter and clamour of Violet's acquisitions, *Heigh-Ho!* were doing their stuff, finding out for the interested public how the new filthy rich were preparing to live their lives.

'I think she likes you,' Emma said, also nodding towards

the house. The windows lit up for an instant as if by an interior electric storm. Which did not, at that moment, seem altogether impossible. The house had a temperature, a humidity, a *climate* of its own.

Emma's Nan had hated the place immediately. 'It's too cold,' she had said.

It was, but that was only the air-conditioning. They'd soon see to it.

But the old girl had a downer on the place before she'd ever clapped eyes on it. Emma and her father soon had her confined to her chair in her own room under a pile of thermally insulating blankets. She complained about not being able to breathe then. She complained non-stop, until only Violet was prepared to listen to her.

But it was very warm in the sunshine reflected from the pool's surface this beautiful morning. The electric storm was raging inside as Emma and her father talked about the very attractive and astute *Heigh-Ho!* Amanda.

'I think she likes you.'

'Who?' Eddie said, but obviously knowing exactly to whom Emma was referring.

'Amanda,' Emma said, playing the game.

Her father grinned. 'Think so?'

'Yes, I do.' She watched him pile egg on to a piece of toast. He sat back, biting into it, pieces of scramble flopping on to his bare belly.

He was wearing a pair of check shorts, white socks and trainers. 'Want some breakfast?' he said.

Emma shook her head. 'I'm not hungry. I'm too excited to eat.'

She felt the warmth of her father's smile. They were like each other. Very. Here they were, living it, exploiting every situation to get what they wanted.

Emma glanced up at him. 'It won't hurt', she said, 'to be nice to people like her.'

'I know,' he said. 'We want all the publicity we can get, don't we?'

o o o

'What's *she* doing here?' Helen hissed.

She and Emma were sitting on the edge of the pool having their photograph taken. They had already been snapped preparing to go in, snapped swimming, towelling themselves, sitting with their feet in the water against the backdrop of the huge, heavily wooded grounds.

Emma had been watching her father talking with Amanda by the ornamental pond, the two of them walking down the manicured lawn deep in conversation. Emma's mother was stuck in the house with old Mrs Green. All those millions in the bank and someone was still having to fix the old girl's food, clear up after her. It didn't make sense. They shouldn't let the old girl do this to them any more. It wasn't necessary. They could afford to pay anyone; real doctors, nurses, anyone.

Emma was so uncomfortable with it. It would stick out incongruously in any magazine photoset. Open the Green's skeleton cupboard and out lurched old ladies like bony sore thumbs.

Helen was hissing, 'What's *she* doing here?'

Emma looked up to see her other guests arriving. What, did Helen think she'd be the only one appearing with her in *Heigh-Ho!*? Emma didn't think so.

'I told you Rob was coming,' she said.

'No you didn't!' Helen said.

'I did. Of course I did.'

'You know you didn't,' Helen said as they stood up together, Emma in her Paris-cut swimsuit, Helen in her standard secondary-school brown. 'Anyway, she's not Rob, is she!'

Emma walked away. She was waving at Rob. Rob and Fidget

were waving back. Claire had stepped back slightly, was glowering in the background.

Emma ran up to them. 'Come in. What do you think?'

'Cool,' Rob said.

Fidget was snapping his fingers at everything at once. The photographer was on him like a shot. Fidget was dancing, space-walking up to the pool.

'He's from *Heigh-Ho!* magazine,' Emma told Rob.

Claire was on to it like a shot. 'What's he doing here? You're never going in *Heigh-Ho!* are you? Are we going in as well? Let's get changed. Where can we get changed? What's she doing here?' Claire said, having noticed Helen in a brown sulk at the other end. 'They wouldn't want to see that in *Heigh-Ho!* surely,' she said.

'Don't be nasty,' Emma laughed. 'You want to have something to be contrasted against, don't you?' Claire laughed too. They both glanced at Helen. Helen, Emma could see, was embarrassed to see them laughing at her. Rob was taking off his shirt. The *Heigh-Ho!* camera went to work.

'In the house,' Emma laughed. 'Get changed in the house.'

'What was she saying about me?' Helen wanted to know, as soon as Emma came back to the pool. The others were in the house, being shown round by Emma's mum.

'Oh, you know what she's like,' Emma said.

'Yes, I know what she's like all right. But what was she saying about me?'

'Oh, leave it, Helen. It isn't worth it.'

Helen was looking into the surface of the pool. 'I need to know', she was saying, 'what she said to you about me, that you both found so funny.'

'Oh – nothing. Not really. Not by her standards. I was laughing at Rob, not at you. I don't know what Claire was doing and I don't care. Just don't involve me, that's all. Chill out.'

'Chill out? Listen to you. You never used to talk like that before –'

'Hey!' Emma called, as the others were coming out of the house in their swimsuits. Claire had a bikini on.

'Look at the state of that,' Helen hissed. 'Look at that fat hanging out. What does she think she looks like?'

'Look at Robbie though,' Emma whispered.

Hey, do look at Rob, though. He looked all right in a pair of longish shorts. He looked – he really looked *Heigh-Ho!* Especially with skinny Fidget by his side like some kind of stick insect.

'Come on then,' Rob called over his shoulder to Fidget and Claire. Emma ran from Helen's side to get to the pool with Rob. Claire was watching, hating it. Emma could feel Claire's hatred. She could feel Helen's hatred of Claire. She and Rob leapt simultaneously into the pool. They surfaced to see Fidget Godman flying through the air like a flung twig. He splatted on to the surface of the water. Emma imagined him being unable to get himself wet, like an insect unable to break the surface tension of the water.

'Is it cold?' Claire was calling to Rob from the side.

'Don't worry about it,' Rob called back. 'Just jump in. Come on.'

'Come on,' Fidget called, 'it's fantastic.' He was thrashing through the water in the same way as he thrashed through the air. His spindly, angular limbs juddered, splashing out in every direction as he front spider-crawled towards where Claire hesitated on the edge.

Claire was over-hesitant, trotting backwards away from the edge. She was turning in circles, stopping, moving forward. 'Is it cold?' she was calling to Rob, again and again, completely ignoring the fact that Fidget was hanging his string-arms over the edge by her feet.

'Is it cold?' she kept calling. Emma could see her glancing and glancing at the *Heigh-Ho!* photographer. Emma noticed

36

Helen watching Claire as she pouted and posed in her bikini without any intention whatsoever of jumping in.

'Is it cold Rob?' Claire called again.

Emma saw the look on Helen's face. She saw that look on Helen's face just before Helen opened her mouth to say, 'Why don't you just face it, Claire – they don't want any pictures of your white disgusting flab.'

Emma ducked under the water, preparing herself.

∘ ∘ ∘

Just as well, because when she surfaced, it had all started.

The *Heigh-Ho!* camera was clicking away on fast-forward automatic as Claire went furious-forward for Helen's throat. Helen was already thrashing, lashing out at anything that might come within her reach. Fidget was slipping out of the pool without a ripple, while Rob was crawling like an Olympic athlete into the affray.

'You little cow!' Claire was screaming.

The droopy mouth of *Heigh-Ho!* curled suddenly into a journalistic smile of approval.

'Come here!' Claire screamed, trying to get through Helen's flying arms.

'Stay away from me!' Helen was shrieking back, her sharp little fists striking home.

Claire was screaming as Fidget got to her, fastening himself round her waist like a tapeworm struggling to hold on. Claire took a flying fist on the chin as she accidentally elbowed Fidget on the nose. A red line appeared down Fidget's chest immediately. He looked, to Emma, making her way out of the pool, like a squeeze of toothpaste with fluoride in the stripe.

Rob arrived, diving between them all. 'Hey! Hey!' he was shouting.

'That cow hit me!' Claire was screaming, trying to shove Rob out of the way. 'She hit me! I'm going to kill her!'

'Let her try!' Helen was shouting. 'Let her try!'

Fidget had gone down on to his knees, blood gushing from his nose. 'Me nose is broken!' he was crying. 'Me nose is broken!'

'Rob! Get out of my way!' Emma watched Claire screaming. 'I'm going to kill her!'

'No you're not!' Rob was saying. 'Calm down, the lot of you. Calm down!'

'Me nose is broken!'

'Let her try, the fat cow!'

'I'll give you fat cow, you skanky swot!'

'Me nose! It's broken!'

'Calm down!'

The camera was snapping, clack clack clack. Fidget screamed red. 'Me nose!' Emma noticed, from the corner of her eye, her father running with *Heigh-Ho!* Amanda across the lawn.

'Let go of me!' Claire shrieked. 'Let go of me!' – shoving Rob from her.

Robbie staggered back, falling over Fidget as he knelt there as if praying. Rob went down as Emma's father came rushing at them, just in time to trip into Rob's legs and take a really quite impressive running dive at the pool. Amanda stood there with her mouth open as Eddie Green disappeared in a huge splash. She stared as he reappeared in an even bigger turmoil, panicking for his life in the deep end.

'He can't swim!' Emma shrieked, adding her own raised voice to the hysteria as Rob kicked Fidget away, as Fidget kicked back and Helen and Claire tussled with each other, falling between the sun-loungers in a mass of bare limbs and shrieks.

'He can't swim!' Emma screamed. The auto-camera was churning as Amanda *Heigh-Ho!* jumped into the pool after Eddie. Rob dived into the tangled web that was Helen and Claire, with a dizzy and bloodied Fidget after him.

Everyone was screaming.

Emma looked at the house. At one of the upstairs windows she saw her mother and her grandmother looking out, horrified. Emma glanced at the two boys and two girls fighting each other. She looked at the pool. A sopping Amanda in green was heaving Eddie Green towards the edge, giving him the kiss of life. Eddie was kissing her back.

At the upstairs window, two faces in horrified bemusement.

Emma's new bedroom.

First part, about the size of the living-room and half the kitchen in their old house. Big double bed, with so much room all the way round it. So much space, Emma couldn't fill it all.

Second part, *en suite* corner Jacuzzi bath with separate shower closet, all with gold taps and gold showerhead fittings.

Joining the two sections, a walk-in wardrobe, a walk-*through* wardrobe into which you could have fitted Emma's old bed, her chest of drawers and her old wardrobes.

Fantastic!

Fitted carpets throughout. A TV set by the bed: remote, sound-system, CD, DVD, the lot. Then, get this, only speakers and a screen in the Jacuzzi room. Luxury? What else can you need?

Except of course, that what you needed to see on opening the hydraulic quadruple-doors of the wardrobe rooms was a full rack both ways. As it stood, whenever Emma passed from bedroom to Jacuzzi or back again, the inadequacy of her few and lonely clothes affronted all the vacant spaces. Dozens of empty hangers clicked and swayed in the cold breeze, waiting to be filled.

o o o

Emma made her way down the stairs the morning after the pool party. In the end, *Heigh-Ho!* had got plenty of pictures of Emma and Rob, after the others had all departed. They'd left bloody-nosed and harried, upset and disgusted, for whatever reasons of their own. Emma couldn't be bothered trying to keep up with it all.

She'd had an argument with Helen when Helen had accused her of starting the trouble on purpose.

'I didn't start the trouble,' Emma had laughed at her, 'you did. You and Claire.'

Helen had gone off in one of her huffs. Emma didn't really mind. Helen was always stomping off for one reason or the other. Emma couldn't be bothered trying to deal with it right now, especially with Rob there and no Fidget and no Claire to get in the way. She could always call Helen later, if she felt like it.

If she felt like it.

Emma and Rob were left gloriously alone with the publicity machine in full flow. In the end, they had between them a great day. A really great day. One of the best of Emma's life. She felt wonderful in front of the *Heigh-Ho!* camera with Rob. She felt right, as if she and he belonged there. They looked the part together. Even Emma's mother had to agree. They looked the part all right. Eddie kept saying so, until Violet eventually had to agree.

Eddie was right there with them. He knew what it was all about, the wealth, the publicity. He knew when something looked right and when it didn't. That's why he agreed so readily with Emma that they should do everything they could to try to keep his mother out of the way. They all loved her and everything, but, anyone could see, she didn't look the part. *Heigh-Ho!* wanted a contrast with the old housing estate, not a hangover from it.

∘ ∘ ∘

. . . Emma came downstairs next day. She had been going through her wardrobe, literally. On the way through, she had to look hard to spot any clothes, dotted as they were amidst the forest of vacant hangers. She shivered on her way to the kitchen. The avenues were long and chill, the air-con grids one continuous arctic hiss on the long trek from one room to the next. She found her mother practising wheeling her grandmother across the expanse of the floor tiles in a brand-new wheelchair.

'Ooh my Gawd!' the old lady was squealing, her wide-eyed head wagging on top of a heap of wrapped blanket.

'Mind out!' she was crying. 'Ooh Gawd! The wheels are coming off! You got any brakes, Vi?' Violet was laughing.

Emma watched them. She had been feeling pretty good, pretty pleased with herself and the way things were going.

She stood watching them.

'Ooh Gawd! Ooh my good Gawd, Vi!'

Violet, roaring with laughter, suddenly looked up and saw her daughter standing there. The smile evaporated from her face. 'Hello, Em,' she said.

Old Mrs Green looked at her granddaughter.

'Your Nan's mobile again,' Violet said, smiling tentatively.

'Oh no I'm not,' Mrs Green was saying. 'You're not going to get me out in this contraption. Out? In this contraption? You're not going to.'

Emma was watching her grandmother.

'What do you think, Em?' her mother said. 'You could take your Nan out in this, couldn't you?'

'Out?' old Mrs Green was saying. 'There's nowhere I want to go, out. Where do I want to go, out?'

Emma's mother was looking at her daughter, as if asking for some support.

Emma shrugged. 'There's nowhere for her to go,' she said, quite simply. 'Where's Dad?'

Violet and old Mrs Green faltered, stalled by Emma's callously simple answer. 'He's in the garden,' Emma's mother told her.

Emma went from the cold stunned silence of the kitchen to the heat and birdsong of the summer garden. 'What you doing, Dad?' she called to Eddie as he was bending over, red-faced by the pool.

He straightened, sweating, breathing heavily. 'I'm exercising,' he stammered, gasping. 'Don't want to get –' he gasped, jogging heavily on the spot, '– fat.' He slapped the falling pot of his belly. 'That's enough –' he said, picking up a pint glass full of orange juice, '– for one day. Don't want to be getting too thin, either,' he said, slapping the pot again, pushing down the waistband of his check shorts. 'Seen your Nan's new wheelchair? GT Turbo. Limited edition. If it isn't the best –' he said, swigging from the glass.

'So,' he said, 'what's wrong with you this morning? Face like a codfish. What are you after?'

Emma started laughing. 'Who says I'm after anything?'

'New house, swimming-pool, an outrageous monthly allowance, face like a codfish. Stands to reason.'

Emma went to hug him. 'Oh, no,' she said, pushing him away. 'You're all sweaty.'

'Hungry, too,' he said. 'Come on, let's go in for breakfast. I'm wasting away, I am.'

'Dad,' Emma said, halting him. 'Before we go. There is one thing.'

'You do surprise me,' he said, smiling.

'Dad, listen. I've been asked – by Rob, you know, who was here yesterday? – he's asked me to go out with him on Friday night.'

'Has he? Where?'

'Only in town. Mallory's.'

'Mallory's? You're not old enough, are you?'

Emma glared at him.

He held up his hands. 'Oh! Sorry! Bad mistake. What am I

saying? – All I meant was, you'd better let your mother know where you're going. That's all.'

Emma smiled once more. 'Thanks, Dad.'

'Is that it then?' he said, making for the house. 'That wasn't much, was it?'

'No, Dad, wait a minute. Listen.'

'I'm listening.'

'I'm going out on Friday –'

'I know. Make sure you tell your mother.'

'Have you seen my wardrobe?'

'No. Have you seen mine?'

'No, Dad, listen. My wardrobe's empty. I'm going out on Friday. With Rob.'

'Ah. With Rob.'

'I haven't got anything good to wear, Dad.'

'Ah.'

'And – remember what you said?'

'Yes. What did I say?'

'New York? Concorde? New York, shopping?'

'Ah – ah!'

o o o

'When?'

'Tomorrow.'

'Tomorrow?'

'Where?' old Mrs Green was screeching over Violet's and Eddie's conversation. 'Where?'

'Tomorrow?' Violet was saying. She was at one of the kitchen sinks, up to her elbows in steaming hot water and a pair of industrial rubber gloves. '*Tomorrow?*' Emma was cringing over the other side of the vast kitchen table. She was glad to be so far away from the rest. So very far away. 'Why tomorrow?'

'Why not?' Eddie shrugged. 'Tomorrow? Next week?'

Emma cringed. She had to, had to, had to go tomorrow. She

was glad she had the expanse of the billiard-table-sized table separating her from the conversation.

'Where's she want to go?' Mrs Green was asking, craning her neck. She was fiddling with the railed wheels of the wheelchair trying to turn herself around, but the chair was going nowhere.

'Next week then,' Violet said, picking another shattered glass out of the washing-up cauldron before her. Emma cringed. She opened her mouth. Her father glanced at her to keep quiet.

He started shaking his head. 'No, can't make it next week. Look at all the engagements I've got, Vi.'

'Engagements?' old Mrs Green croaked, her head straining round almost one hundred and eighty degrees.

'Well I don't have any engagements next week, but I'm not going to New York tomorrow, Concorde or no Concorde,' Violet said, peering through her steamed-up glasses. The cold water ran hot in this house. The hot simply spat boiled water vapour into the bowl.

'Where?' old Mrs Green strained and said. She was wearing a safety belt like an abseiler's harness in her wheelchair. 'Where you not going, Vi?'

'New York, Mum,' Violet snapped at her.

'Where?'

'New York!' Eddie almost shouted. 'The States! New York!'

'America?' the old girl yodelled, turning to peer at Violet. 'America? I'm not having no strangers, Vi. I'm not.'

'No, I know you're not, Mum.'

Emma was squirming.

'Who's going to America then? I'm not going to America!'

'No, Mum!' Eddie bellowed. 'We are! Me and Em!'

'I'm staying here with you, Mum,' Vi said.

'When you coming back?' Mrs Green said.

'On Wednesday,' Eddie told her.

'I don't want to go, anyway,' Violet was saying.

'Oh no you're not,' Mrs Green said, her head passing from one side to the other, 'not to America and back in two days you're not!'

'Oh, yes we are,' Eddie said, winking at Emma.

Emma was breathing a hot sigh of relief. Her mother was filling one of the kettles. Emma watched her arm shaking under the weight of it. 'Why anyone would want to go all that way for two days is beyond me,' she was saying. She shuddered, as if in horror. 'I don't even like going out any more.'

'No, nor do I,' Emma's Nan said. 'I know exactly what you mean, Vi. I know exactly what you mean.'

o o o

'Somebody's got to do it,' Violet said, with her head in the cupboard. 'Some of us don't get the time to go running off to America, some of us don't.'

Emma was trying to eat her breakfast. She was so excited she could hardly swallow. First it was Paris, now, suddenly, New York. Where next? Eddie had gone back to bed after the exertion of his exercises by the pool. Emma was trying to talk to her mother about their trip and about going to Mallory's with Rob. But her mother's head and half her torso were stuffed into the kitchen cabinets.

Old Mrs Green was letting out squeaking noises from the depths of her cladding. It was as if she couldn't exhale properly in her sleep without the weight of her wrappings squeezing the air out of her like a long bagpipes.

'Is Nan okay?' Emma was asking. She was eating toast and jam with butter chips carved from the block, and flame-thrown toast burnt black but scraped over the sink. Everything in the house seemed programmed to over-function, as if the electricity was squirting in too hard or too fast. The ionised, high-tension air gathered dust from miles around. The deep-pile carpets all stood abruptly on end whenever something else was switched on, relaxing again a few moments later. Gangs of utensils, liquidisers and vacuum cleaners lurked in the corners, threatening to be used.

Emma's mother had discovered shopping on the Internet. Emma suspected Violet of doing something stupid on someone's PC. Cleaning equipment kept arriving at their door, surprising everyone, including Violet, with the increasing regularity of the deliveries.

Emma's grandmother was squeaking, squeezed under layer upon layer. 'Is Nan all right?' Emma asked.

Her mother was climbing into the cupboard under the sinks. Emma could see just the backs of her legs sticking out. 'I can't hear you!' she was shouting.

Emma was trying to eat her toast. It tasted all wrong. It had a suspicious after-flavour, like detergent, or ammonia. 'Maybe things taste better with a few germs on them,' she tried saying to the backs of her mother's legs, as her mother clattered about like something in a box. 'Mum?' Emma said. 'You know I'm going out on Friday, when we get back from New York, don't you?'

'What? I can't hear you. I'm trying to clean this bit in here. Nobody's cleaned this bit in here.'

Emma watched her. Or watched her legs, at least. The calves above the socks were very still. They seemed to hang there, belonging to no one. It looked like you could pull them away, as if they'd become detached and her mother had gone on without them, a legless grub worming its way through the underbelly of the house.

Emma had a sudden image of a maggot in a fallen apple. 'Mum?' she said. The dislocated legs made no reply. Emma's Nan whistled through the magnetic hum of the house. 'Mum?'

Nothing stirred. Violet's violet socks sagged softly round the surprisingly thin ankles. Her calves, as Emma turned to concentrate on them, appeared like sticks stripped clean of bark, shining, with a slow, varicose depth.

'Mum? Are you all right?' There was no answer. 'Mum?' Emma said, standing up. She went to the cupboard under the sink, looked up her mother's body.

Violet was lying with her face turned to the side. The clasped hand nearly touching the tip of her nose was clutching the kitchen cloth. One corner of the cloth seemed to have found its way into Violet's mouth.

'Mum?' Emma said, touching one of her heels through the purple pop-sock.

Violet's eyes opened. Her head came up. 'What's the matter?' she said, looking down the line of her body at her daughter.

'Are you all right, Mum?'

'All right? Course I'm all right. Why?'

'I thought – for a minute –'

Emma was peering at her mother's long thin face tucked away in the gloom of the cupboard under one of the sinks in the massive kitchen. The face blinked down at her, with the bleary-eyed expression of someone just waking from a sudden and unexpected sleep.

Emma breezed into Mallory's trying to look as if she did it all the time. The place was packed. It was really something. There was a little dance floor.

She caught sight of herself in the mirrors behind the bar. She looked eighteen at least. Nineteen even. She looked pretty wild. Her hair was done so that it looked scruffy, but cost a hundred pounds a time to look like that.

'A hundred pounds?' her dad had laughed. 'Is that all? Are you sure they're doing it right?'

Emma's dad was quickly changing his mind about champagne. He had been a home-brew beer drinker, but not any longer. 'If it's not the best,' he'd become very fond of saying, 'then it's not worth having.'

Emma looked eighteen easily when she walked into Mallory's on her own. She was looking this way and that, looking everywhere to be certain that Claire Thomas hadn't got there before her. Catching sight of herself in the mirror behind the bar, she saw a stranger passing by where she would normally have been. The stranger was a young woman, full of a confidence that belied the truth of the nervous fear turning Emma's stomach. Still, that was what make-up was for, as far as she was concerned.

No sign of Claire.

She saw Fidget Godman nod at Rob as she walked through the busy, crowded bar. Rob turned as she crossed the small dance floor to where he and Fidget stood beside the little stage on which the record decks were set.

Rob turned as she crossed the floor. Chart music was being played. A screen with coloured images illuminated

Rob's background. He turned as Emma walked towards him.

She almost, almost stalled, her stomach churning so much she felt as if she needed to rush for the loo. She hadn't seen him since the pool party. Now here she was, turning up on him like this, on her own, here specifically to see him. She felt slightly sick, or as if she was about to let out a huge burp.

But Rob turned and looked at her. With his face against the changing background colours of the screen, he smiled.

Emma caught her breath. He smiled that smile. *That smile*. He was very, very good looking. Everyone fancied Robbie Britto.

He smiled at Emma and changed her bubble of indigestion instantly into a flutter of excitement. She crossed that little dance floor on flying feet, almost rushing into him as he held out is hand for her.

'Hey!' he called, almost shouting to make himself heard above the music. 'I'm glad you could make it. Have you come on your own?'

Emma nodded, smiling back into his face. She couldn't speak, she felt so nervous and excited. She felt like laughing. There *was* no one else she could have come with. No one else was up to her standards.

'We're starting our set soon,' Robbie shouted at her. 'Let me get you a drink before we start.' Emma nodded again. She let Rob lead her over to the bar, calling hello to Fidget Godman on the way past. She indicated his nose by touching her own then pointing at his. Fidget was clicking and trembling over the record boxes, his hands fluttering a brief hello back. He raised his eyebrows in recognition, holding up his thumbs before turning a full three hundred and sixty degrees on the stage.

Emma laughed. 'He's pretty crazy,' she said to Rob as they got to the bar.

'Who, Fidge?' Rob said, glancing back.

Emma could see the affection and respect in Rob's face. 'No he's not,' he said, smiling back at Emma, 'he's completely crazy. He's pure MC. You wait till you hear him.' Rob was shaking his head. 'No one can talk that fast. Not like he does it, anyway. What would you like to drink?'

Emma stood near the crowded bar with Robbie Britto. There she was standing in Mallory's, actually in Mallory's, at the bar, while Robbie Britto, *Robbie Britto*, was buying her a drink.

It was too like a dream to be true.

Rob gave her an orange juice. 'Sure you wouldn't prefer something in that?' he said. Emma shook her head. 'Listen,' he said, 'we're just about to start. Brilliant timing. Don't go away.'

'Oh, I won't,' Emma said.

'I'm relying on you,' Rob said. 'You got to dance, right?'

'What?'

'Dance. Get 'em going. Will you do it? I'm relying on you.'

There was a whole bar full of people, and Rob was asking her to dance by herself on the deserted dance floor. Emma looked about self-consciously. 'Oh, I don't know,' she breathed. 'I don't know if I can. Not just like –'

'Of course you can. Come on. Please. You're a brilliant dancer. Come on, be bold. What's happened to you since last week?'

Emma looked again at the crowd. What had happened to her since last week? New York, New York! There she and Eddie had been treated like the King of Europe and his daughter. New York, where money was properly respected. Let there be no mistake, New York City was what had happened to Emma since last week. She loved it. She and her father had lived it. They had met – you'll never guess who they'd met. Nobody would believe her. Nobody would. They'd only met –

'What's happened to you since last week?'

Emma took a deep breath. Movie stars. Movie stars'

beautiful wives. 'I'll dance', she said, 'if you'll come shopping with me in London next week.'

Rob, smiling, jumped up on the stage. The chart music faded out. Fidget already had the microphone. The whole place paused, with everyone looking up and over, craning to see what was happening.

Rob looked about. Fidget juddered into gear. Rob turned one of the decks. The needle made contact. The disk flew backwards and forwards under Rob's hand. Sound started up out of everywhere. The new music beat out so much bass Emma could feel it in her chest. Fidget started speaking over the bass beat, his words flying, his nervous free hand fluttering. He was stalking up and down as Rob mixed another tune into his compare.

Everyone in the whole bar was watching Rob and Fidget on the stage. It was a real gig, a proper performance. Emma saw Rob glance at her. She swallowed her juice, left the empty glass on the bar. She moved forward towards the dance floor, taking off her jacket as she went. She dumped the thousand-pound jacket in a corner as she stepped into the coloured lights.

Rob was smiling at her. Fidget was absolutely manic there on the stage as Emma started to move. She moved. Did she ever. In front of the whole bar full of people, she danced on her own, feeling it, wanting it, loving it.

They all knew who she was now. She felt them recognising her. There was no mistake. She had arrived. This was what she was about. This, and more. So much, so much more.

Yes. She had arrived. And this was only the beginning.

o o o

In the end, she had to leave. She hadn't been able to tell her mother where she was going. Her mother wasn't like Eddie: she wouldn't have understood.

But Emma was exhausted anyway, dancing herself into a

trance and back. She was, at one point, flying. She was somewhere else. It was fantastic. Emma had never known anything like it.

She was perfect. Beautiful. Everyone was watching her. She wanted them to, and they did. They did what she wanted them to do.

That's exactly how she felt. As if she could get people to do whatever she wanted. At one point, she indicated, merely indicated to a man at the bar that she wanted something to drink. She wanted water. Somehow, that's exactly what he brought her. In a little plastic bottle. As if she could have got him to do anything she wanted. Anything.

You should have seen the jealousy on the faces of the girls in the crowd. They hated her. Literally hated her. Good. That's what she wanted of them. She was not like them, not at all.

Rob was with her, all the way. He understood exactly what she was going through. Emma could feel him with her. All alone on the dance floor, she was not all alone, but dancing to Robbie's music. She was dancing to Rob's tune.

So was Fidget. His words fitted exactly into the spaces left for him by Rob. Words and music, music and dance. It all fitted, woven out of Rob's understanding of what Fidget Godman and Emma Green could do.

In the end, some of the jealous girls tried to compete with Emma on the little dance floor. But they were pale shadows, nobodies like Claire Thomas with nothing to offer but their teensy small-town preferences and petty hatreds.

Emma didn't know any of them, nor did she wish to. She wanted to be noticed. She wanted to be noticed by Rob, by everyone. She succeeded. She danced until it was time for her to leave. Claire didn't show. Or if she had, Emma hadn't seen her. She hoped she had turned up. She'd have taken one look at Emma on the dance floor and disappeared again, back home, tail firmly between her legs.

Emma knew when it was time for her to go, not by the clock, but by the numbers of dancers on the floor. Too many had stopped noticing her. She was reduced by the crowd filling up her floor space. Down among the others, she could possibly have been de-elevated to the level of any of the office girls or young typists out to blow their first week's wages.

All at once, she picked up the wretched heap that was her jacket, waved goodbye to Rob and Fidget and went for the door. The boys waved back. Rob blew her a kiss, which she caught.

Walking, sailing, through the darkened crowd, she could see the eyes focused upon her. She felt the crowds slightly separate as she passed through. Emma Green felt the power of her command.

Outside, she looked up at the clear sky and laughed. It was a warm night. The trodden coat she carried weighed heavy. So she dropped it in the middle of the pavement as she went.

She ignored the voice that called out to her as she made her way to the cab-office. Let them all call to her. She could do whatever she liked. One of the jealous office girls could have her discarded jacket for all she cared. It would be the best thing in any of that lot's wardrobe, easily. Emma's cast-offs were better than anything they could ever hope to have.

'Go for it, girl,' her dad had taken to saying. He wanted her to have the best. She'd put up with the inferior for all her life, so why not? Her father had said he'd always known that they were better. They *were* better. Emma had been elevated so suddenly into the better position that she could still see her old self on the ground scrabbling with all the others. But that old self was fading, and fading fast.

o o o

'Go for it, girl,' her dad had taken to saying.

And yet when Emma came flying in from Mallory's, her feet way off the ground, her head full of new images and future experiences, there he was; her dad, definitely not going for it.

Sailing in, hungry, thirsty, excited, everything, Emma found him slouched at the far kitchen table, a coat thrown across his shoulders against the cold, a glass of bubbly slowly flattening on the table in front of him. Emma turned on the lights as she entered, seeing her father there as a sky-full of strip lighting flickered and buzzed overhead.

Eddie blinked in the blaze of new light, surprised to be discovered not going for it like this, with his coat draped limply over his sloping shoulders. Emma caught sight of him way off across the kitchen, like a figure photographed from this distance to capture the full, pathetic effect.

'Emma,' he blinked over at her, squinting through the blank white blaze. 'How you doing, Em?'

'Dad. I'm all right. I'm good. What are you doing sitting in the dark?'

He shrugged. 'Thinking. You know.'

Emma went over to him. He looked into the effervescent glass on the table before him. 'Shall I make you a cup of tea or something?' she said.

'No,' he said, 'I'm fine with this. Champagne celebration, innit.'

Emma drew up a chair and sat next to him. 'Are you all right, Dad?'

He breathed in deeply, touching his wine glass without picking it up. 'Me? Yeah. Of course. I'm fine – anyway, look at you, you look great.'

Emma beamed. 'I've been out. To Mallory's. Remember?'

'Oh, yes,' he said. 'How was it? You look pretty pleased with yourself. I bet it was good. I'd have loved to've seen you. Did your mother – did she know where you were going? – Emma? Did you tell her?'

Emma was pulling faces. 'Nearly. I nearly told her.'

'Nearly? How can you nearly tell somebody something?'

'I was going to tell her, Dad, really, I was. But she – it's like, she –'

'You didn't tell her, did you?'

'No, Dad.'

'You couldn't, could you?'

'No. She wasn't – she was falling asleep. In the cupboard.'

'Yeah,' he said. 'I know.'

Emma was looking at him as he stared into the bubbles climbing the sides of the champagne glass. 'Dad? – You knew she was falling asleep in the cupboard? *You knew*?'

He was nodding. 'She's up most the night counting.'

'Counting? Counting what?'

'Photographs. Bits of paper. Laying things in drawers.'

'Laying things in drawers? What do you mean?'

He looked up at her. He took a very, very deep breath. 'Ever since we moved. She has dreams. She gets up and looks in drawers. She touches everything. Then she closes the drawer, then opens it again, and touches everything again. She falls asleep in cupboards. I have to dig her out of the wardrobe every morning.'

'Oh. Is she all – what's the matter with her?'

'I don't know. It's this house,' he said, looking about. 'I don't know. She won't go out any more. She feels – she thinks everyone's watching her.'

'What's wrong with that?' Emma said, thinking about dancing on her own all evening in Mallory's.

'Nothing. Nothing's wrong with it, Em, not for you or me. It's good, isn't it?'

'Yes,' Emma said, without any hesitation.

'Yes,' he said, 'it's really good. We love it, you and me, don't we? We were made for it, I reckon, don't you?'

'I reckon so, Dad,' Emma said.

Her dad turned and put his arms round her shoulders. She touched his padded sides with her open hands. 'We were made for it, we were,' he whispered.

They stayed there for a minute, for two minutes, before Emma said, 'She'll get used to it. It's all the changes, all at once.'

'Yeah,' her father said, sighing. He turned and picked up his wine glass. 'Anyway. Champagne Charlie, that's me. I just ordered a white Roller.'

'Fantastic!' Emma smiled. 'Then, you're not going to let it – stop you, in any way, Dad, are you?'

He looked straight at her. 'Your mum's complaining about the new car.'

'Dad,' Emma said, 'we were made for it, weren't we?' They were looking into each other's eyes.

'And your Nan,' he said. 'She's not at all well.' Still Emma looked closely at him. There was a long, long pause.

'There's this,' he started to say, then stopped. He thought about it. 'I know someone,' he said, 'who's looking for a partner, a half-share in a bar.'

'A bar?'

'Yeah. In Spain. A bar in Spain. She's – they're just looking for some finance. It'll be great fun. I really fancy it.' He stopped. Emma watched his face as he looked at her. Still he didn't say anything.

'You're not going to let anything stop you, Dad,' Emma said, quietly, 'are you?'

Eddie glanced round, as if to be sure nobody was listening. 'I'll have to, you know, go out there for a while.'

Emma watched his little, pensive smile. She too looked behind to see if anyone was there. There was no one. They were alone, together in this. Emma didn't want him to have to go anywhere. But if you were made for money, like Eddie and Emma, you had to do these things. You had to make things happen. She looked back at him. His face told her he was waiting, just waiting to be told of her approval. 'We were made for it, Dad. I've been to Mallory's, with Rob.'

They both looked round as something, some automatic

utensil or control system clicked on. The new grinding sound soon settled into the background hum of the kitchen. Emma and her father hunkered down, more closely-knit, more confidential.

'I've been to Mallory's. I had a great time. It's out there, Dad. It's really out there. All we've got to do is go for it.'

Her father smiled. 'Champagne Charlie,' he said.

That night, Emma couldn't sleep. She was too excited, thinking about dancing in Mallory's with Rob and everyone else watching her. She was too excited – but, somehow, her excitement felt a little like being afraid.

Her bed was too big. It didn't seem to have any edges, any boundaries to stick to. She seemed to have just too much room to move about. The more room there was, the more difficult it was proving to find a place to rest.

Her life seemed like that, at the moment. All the boundaries had disappeared. Which, she supposed, must be a good thing. All the old constraints had been blown away. The old bed was at the town dump, where it belonged; where it had belonged for years. The new bed was a vast expanse in a powerfully huge room. She'd grow into it, one day. She would have to, because she was here now. This was it, her life.

But she couldn't help remembering being a much smaller child tucked firmly into her old bed. She kept remembering the smells and the sounds of their old house, being warm in bed when it was horrible and raining outside.

Now it only seemed to be horrible weather inside; it was so cold all the time. Now it sounded false, like the inside of a machine. If she listened out for her mother counting things, or laying things in drawers, or for the sound of her grandmother's incessant grumble, all she could hear was the rumble and thrum of a distant engine. She was just too excited, she supposed; that was why things didn't feel right. She felt a bit unsettled, like her mother. That was only natural. So many things were changing all at once.

She thought of Helen. She thought of the nice times she

and her friend had shared, sleeping over in each other's houses. If Helen were here now, she thought, she'd feel different. It would all be so much better. Helen hadn't called since the pool party. Emma had wanted to let her sulk. But perhaps, she was thinking, she should give her a call in the morning? Helen was, after all, still her best friend.

o o o

'You're what? I don't believe it!' Helen wasn't saying anything. 'You're what? What did you say?'

'I think you heard me,' Helen said.

'You're going shopping – with Claire?'

'Yes.'

'With Claire Thomas?'

'Yes.'

Emma didn't know what to say. She was stuck for words, struck dumb with the telephone to her ear, sitting in the sun by the pool. 'Let me get this straight,' Emma said. 'You, Helen, are going shopping today, with Claire – with Claire Thomas?'

'Yes. Why? Is that really so difficult for you to understand?'

'Well yes, it is, as a matter of fact.'

'Well,' Helen snapped back, 'as a matter of fact we are. And we're going to enjoy ourselves without having to spend hundreds of pounds on some dress.'

'Oh,' Emma said, 'that's what it is, is it?'

'No,' Helen said, 'that is not what it is. What it is, is I don't want to come round because you've got a pool and because you've got a bigger house than me and you think you've got a better –'

'Helen, I didn't mean it like that. I just thought –'

'No, Emma, you didn't think. You seem to have stopped thinking, unless you're worrying about buying everything in sight or going to the pub with Robbie Britto.'

'Ah!' Emma exclaimed. 'I can hear Claire talking now,' she said, 'but she's using your voice.'

'Don't be stupid,' Helen said.

'Don't you call me stupid,' Emma snapped.

'You are stupid. I used to think Claire was stupid and a user, but now I think it's you. I really do.'

Emma, breathing into the telephone, could hear Helen breathing into the other end. 'Well,' Emma said, deliberately, 'let me tell you something you can go and tell Claire Thomas. The two of you are well suited to each other. You're both a couple of losers. You're in the past, both of you. I've moved on. You understand me? Helen? Hey! Don't you hang up on me!' she found herself yelling into the dead handset.

She threw down the telephone.

The nerve!

Helen and Claire. Claire and Helen. Emma stood up and kicked one of the garden chairs over. She ignored the rap on the window behind her. She'd show them. The losers. Ganging up on her like that!

She'd show them. She didn't need them. She was going out on Friday. With Rob. That's what Claire couldn't stand. Emma picked up the garden chair. She smiled. Her mother was looking at her from one of the kitchen windows. Why should she care what Claire Thomas thought or did? She was the one going shopping with Robbie Britto on Friday afternoon, then on to Mallory's with him later. Why should she care?

o o o

'Oh, no you're not!'

'What's she not doing, Vi?' Mrs Green looked up and said.

'Why not? You can't stop me.'

'Yes I can,' Emma's mother said, a loaded spray polish can in her hand. 'You're too young, Emma. You're too young. It's a pub.'

'What's a pub, Vi?' Emma's grandmother said, letting fly with another spray, firing it much further than she could possibly reach from her wheelchair.

'But I only drank some orange juice and some water.'

'I don't care,' Emma's mum said, wiping up after her mother-in-law. 'It's a pub, you're too young. Dancing on your own! It's like you're drunk, even if you're not. There're drugs down there. I've heard –'

Emma's grandmother looked up in terror.

'Mum!' Emma cried. 'It isn't like that at all!'

'It doesn't matter. That's what people say. You're getting yourself talked about, my girl, that's what I care about. You're too young.'

'Don't keep saying that!'

'It's true! You've only just got your GCSE results. You're still at school.'

'Oh, you noticed then, did you?'

'What?'

'Well you didn't seem all that concerned. Not when you found out about the money.'

'That's not true!'

'Isn't it?'

'No, I didn't – it wasn't –'

'I don't care anyway!' Emma almost shouted. Her Nan tutted.

'It doesn't matter. You were right. It's the money. It changes everything.'

'No! You're still a schoolgirl. You've got your –'

'What? You have to be joking!'

'What do you mean?'

'School? What's school got to do with anything?'

'It's got everything to do with everything. What did you think you were going to do with yourself?'

'I'm going to do whatever I want to do. Where's Dad?'

'I don't know, do I? He's not going to stick up for you. He's not here. There are cars everywhere, and another one on order. There's no room left in the garage for any Rolls Royce.'

Emma's grandmother was attempting to shake her head. 'No more room,' she was saying.

Emma glanced at her. 'But it's a *Rolls Royce*! He's got to have a Roller. He has to!'

Emma's mother looked as if she had a bad taste in her mouth. 'He doesn't need all those cars. You can only drive one car at a time.'

'*You* can't even drive that, Vi,' old Mrs Green suddenly said.

'No, Mum. You're right. They're none of them for me, all those cars. You're right there Mum, you are.'

'Why don't you learn to drive, then?' Emma said to her mother.

'Why don't you learn to speak to people properly?' her mother said.

Emma's grandmother tutted again. 'Tell her, Vi,' she clicked.

'I will and all, Mum,' Violet said to her. 'Somebody's got to – where are you going? Emma! Where are you going? Come here!'

'I'm not listening to this,' Emma was saying, making her way out of one of the back doors. 'I don't have to listen to any of this.'

Her mother was trying to follow after her. 'You have to listen if I tell you you're not going to any more pubs. You have to listen to me. You're not old enough! You are just not old enough!' she was calling, stopping before she got to the door that Emma had just left by.

Emma slammed the door. She was stamping through the full and furious sunlight. Her eyes were aching because she hadn't slept properly. The house didn't seem to want to let her sleep. It hummed and throbbed in her ear. Then she had to get up so late and listen to all of her mother's claptrap, with her grandmother like a confused conscience on her mother's shoulder.

It was Friday again. She'd waited all week for this. All week stuck on her own in that house. Now, at last, she was going out. She was going out with Rob and wasn't about to let anything, or anybody spoil it for her.

o o o

Five thousand pounds.

The man in the bank raised his eyebrows. 'Five thousand?'

Emma nodded. Her heart was pounding. Five thousand pounds a minute. 'My mother called yesterday to make the arrangement,' she said. She hadn't. Emma had faked the call herself.

He gazed curiously at her. 'Cash?' he said.

'Yes, please,' Emma said, standing as easy as she could. She looked back at him, as if withdrawing five thousand notes was something she did practically every day. She watched as he went away and checked everything. Yes, it was her account. Yes, she did have that amount of money in it. Easily. Yes, they had received a telephone call. He couldn't stop her, could he?

Emma shifted uncomfortably as he came back to his seat behind the counter. He took a moment to look up at her. She felt all her tiredness return for a moment while he so closely scrutinised her.

'What do you want the money for?' he said.

'What?' she said, astonished. As if it was any of his business! 'What?'

'We need to know you're not a money launderer.'

Emma had a picture of leaving all the money stuffed in her jeans going through the washing-machine. She must have looked confused.

'We need something for our records,' the man said. 'Just tell us what you're going to use the money for.'

'For fun,' Emma told him.

He looked carefully at her again. Emma could see the sudden recognition in his face. She saw his expression saying

Emma Green, of course. *That* Emma Green. 'How would you like the money?' he said, finally.

Emma stared at him. She had a new bag on her back. It was a koala bear. A real one, practically. It looked like a real bear clinging to her. 'You could put it in this,' she said. She watched him stifle a smile.

'What notes would you like?' he said. 'I suppose we'd better try and give you fifties, for this amount.'

'Yes. Try and give me fifties.' She hurried out, feeling on her back the eyes of everyone in the bank. She had the five thousand in fifties stuffed into the clinging koala.

It was strange, walking up the road in her designer sportswear, going to meet Rob with that amount of money in her bag. A weird feeling, but very exciting. It was very exciting just going to meet Rob. He was something else, really. The way he looked. And he was, like, nearly nineteen. Everyone liked him, everyone. Robbie Britto. Emma just loved his name. Everything.

Then when you saw him. Something else! Like, with him just standing there waiting for her, waiting only for her. *Robbie Britto*!

She saw him up the road, waiting for her. Just, simply, standing there waiting for her. She was so excited. She ran up to meet him.

'Hey,' he called, smiling.

Hey. Yeah. He looked – *Italian*. Emma was late, and Rob was smiling. So nice. So good looking.

'I'm sorry,' she started to say.

'Hey,' he said, 'what you sorry for? I don't mind waiting.'

Emma couldn't keep the smile from her face. So what if Helen didn't like her any more? So what if Claire hated her? That was good. She hated Claire. Rob was worth it. To have him smile like that, even when you'd kept him waiting.

They were all jealous. Claire was, for sure. Helen had been

right, she was a user. A loser, too. As if she'd ever been interested in Fidget Godman. *As if*! He was better off without her. She was *such* a user.

'I've been somewhere,' Emma said to Rob.

They started to walk up the road together. Robbie had managed to get the afternoon off work. 'Where do you want to go?' he said.

'Nowhere,' Emma said. 'Just somewhere we can talk. I want to show you something.'

'What?' he said.

'Just something. Let's go to the park or somewhere. It's a surprise. Come on.'

Robbie started running. Emma had to struggle to keep up with him. He said he couldn't wait to get there. He loved surprises, he said. Emma laughed. Rob was something else, really. He was lovely, funny, good-looking. Dead fit. Emma took the koala bag from her back.

'What's the surprise?' Rob said.

Emma went to the empty wooden seat just off the path. She looked to be sure nobody else was within eye or earshot. She untied the backpack, held it open on her lap.

'Look,' she said. Rob peered into it. He seemed to kind of tut, with a click that came from the back of his throat. 'Five thousand,' Emma said.

Rob looked up at her. He looked left and right, as if to ensure also that there was nobody else around to see this amount of money. Rob was blinking, slowly, trying to take in what was being shown to him. Emma sat on the bench looking at him as he looked up at the blue sky, as he peered over the tops of the park's trees to somewhere else entirely. 'I don't believe it,' he said, at length.

Emma was laughing. 'Believe it. Five thousand pounds. All in one go.' She closed the bag. 'Come on,' she said, 'let's go and have some fun.'

o o o

What would you do if you were going to get eighty thousand pounds to spend? If you had a bank account that already had twenty K in it, with plenty more where that came from, what would you do?

You'd be out, wouldn't you? Out like crazy in the city with people like Robbie Britto to help you spend it. You'd be doing the shops like you've never done them. If you saw something you liked, you'd just buy it. No need to see how much it costs. Another handful of paper from your bag, it's yours.

That's what Emma did. She was out. She was rife in the London designer outlets, or slumming it up Oxford Street buying herself anything she liked. CDs, clothes, watches, earrings. Buy that one, have it delivered, get another. Might as well. Buy that one. Buy two. Buy in bulk, there's nothing to stop you. Money can be made quicker than it can be spent, so why not spend it?

All the money from Emma's old house sale was going to be deposited in her own bank account for her to do with as she pleased. For now, she had the twenty thousand to be going on with, so she was pleased. But the only thing was, Rob wasn't fully with her in it. She wanted to buy things for him, good, expensive things. Emma wanted to get him everything he couldn't normally afford. Which was practically everything. Working in his dad's café didn't give him too much money to play with.

But he wouldn't allow her to buy him the things she knew he really wanted. Good clothes. A gold chain. Emma knew he wanted them really. Who wouldn't?

'Let me get it for you,' she said to him time and again. 'Let me get it for you,' as they stood outside an expensive jeweller's looking at the designer watches. 'It's the genuine article,' Emma said, trying to get him just to enter the shop with her.

'I can't,' he said.

'Why not? Of course you can.'

'I can't. Where would I tell my dad I got it from?'

Emma looked puzzled. 'From me, of course. Where else?'

Robbie shook his head. 'I can't. You can buy me lunch though, if you like. I'm starving, aren't you?'

Emma was trying to ignore her feelings of disappointment and frustration. She took Rob into the most expensive restaurant she could find and ordered ordinary fish and chips with tomato sauce and salad cream and pickled onions, with chocolate ice-cream to follow.

At the end of the meal, Emma picked up her ice-cream bowl and licked it. She laughed at Rob's embarrassment, then did it again. Rob laughed and looked around. Everyone was watching them.

'Go on,' Emma whispered to him.

Everyone was watching as Rob picked up his bowl. He licked it, looking over the rim at Emma all the while.

She felt a flood of relief.

The waiter hurried over with their bill. Emma and Rob laughed.

o o o

After the restaurant, Emma went and bought an old-fashioned top hat from an old-fashioned gentlemen's outfitter. Rob was laughing and laughing. This was mad, they both knew. But to Emma, it was also special, because *she* was. And *he* was, being finally here with her, laughing at what she was doing. He was being included, allowing himself to be included in Emma's insane new world.

Claire Thomas couldn't do anything like this. This was sheer Emma Green, with Robbie Britto by her side laughing. She loved making him laugh. His face looked so very – it had to be said – he was beautiful. His eyes. His smile. He emboldened her before the crowds passing in the street.

Without him to endorse her behaviour, Emma couldn't have acted like that, wearing the top hat and dancing like a mime-artist in the street.

An old tramp was watching Emma from a closed shop doorway. Emma did a dance for him. Rob was creasing up.

'Got any spare change?' the old fellow asked her.

'Look at the state of him,' Rob said.

Emma looked up the street. She smiled. 'I know,' she said. 'Come on. Bring him up here. Come on up here, with us,' she said to the old man.

They guided him back to the top-hat shop. There they had him got up in classic pin stripes, a new silk shirt, red patterned tie, socks, underpants (for a change), new leather shoes and a cashmere overcoat. His tragic hair hung in dirty strings across the new clean collars.

The men in the shop were very sniffy about having to do it, to kit out this dirty old tramp. Very sniffy. Well, the old boy's clothes did reek a fair bit. One of the men had to wrap them up and carry them away, throwing them out the back into the bins.

But there was no denying the colour of Emma's money. If she was willing to pay over six hundred pounds to have an old vagrant got up like that, then these were the men to do it. They called the old man Sir. They called Emma Madam, and Rob Sir too. Rob and Emma were stalking about like royalty. Every so often they would lose it, falling about in fits of laughter.

When he was finished, or as finished as he could be without a bath, a razor and a barber, the old fellow stood himself upright in front of the mirror. He was surprisingly tall. 'You know, this reminds me . . .' he said, speaking for the first time, losing himself in some far-off memory.

Rob looked at Emma. She at him. She liked the look on his face. She *loved* the look on his face. It was as if he'd done something today, as if they'd done it together.

Outside, inspecting the old fellow in the light, he wiped his bearded lips with the back of his hand and said, 'How's about a little drink now then?'

Emma and Rob looked at each other. Rob shrugged.

They took the tramp to an off-licence. He was after a huge great bottle of whisky. Instead, they bought him a small bottle and a couple of cans of strong beer. Rob wanted to get him some food, but he said that wouldn't be necessary. 'Some smokes will do,' he insisted.

People stared at the old alcoholic on the pavement sipping whisky politely from a bottle, waving down the street. Emma could see them astonished to see such a perfectly dressed man collapsed across the pavement drinking from a beer can.

Down the street a way, a young beggar in a blanket asked them for any spare change. Emma shoved a handful of notes at him. He backed off in frightened suspicion.

Emma laughed. She walked up to a perfect stranger, a man making his way up the road. She offered him some money. 'Here,' she said.

He skirted round her, a puzzled and perplexed expression on his face. 'Isn't money weird?' Emma said to Rob. He was standing with a kind of half-smile, watching her. 'I mean, it's like, like nothing, isn't it?' Rob was nodding. 'No,' Emma said, 'it is, isn't it? It's like – it doesn't exist. It's a – what is it? Something else. An anomaly. I don't know –'

'You don't know what you're talking about,' Rob said, 'do you?'

'No,' she agreed, laughing. 'I don't know what I'm talking about. Look,' she said, her hands stuffed full of banknotes, 'what happens to this stuff? What do people do? Look,' she said, offering the money to a girl about her own age, 'why don't you want it?'

'What's wrong with her?' the girl said to Rob.

Rob was shrugging. 'I don't know,' he said. 'What's wrong with you, Emma?'

'There's something strange,' Emma said, 'something really strange. I can't put my finger on it. It's something I don't – I can't quite define. It is as if it doesn't exist. It's nothing, this,' she said, holding up the notes. 'This isn't it. It isn't really real. That's it! *It isn't real.*'

'Yeah?' Rob said. 'You try telling that to someone who doesn't have any. Try telling that to my dad.'

'Doesn't your dad have any money?'

'He struggles, you know?'

'The café does all right, doesn't it? He pays you, doesn't he?'

Rob shrugged. 'I don't want to talk about it. Come on. It's nearly time to go.'

'Time to go? Why time to go? It's early yet, isn't it?' Rob was watching her. He looked concerned, slightly confused. 'Well, what time is your gig tonight?' Emma asked. 'We're going together, aren't we?' But Rob still had that confused look on his face 'What's the matter?' she said.

'I thought,' he said softly, 'I thought you knew.'

'Knew? Knew what?'

'Ah . . . I thought you knew – about the phone call.'

'What phone call?'

'The phone call to my dad, this morning?'

Emma was looking hard at him. 'Phone call from who, might I ask?' she asked.

Rob hesitated. 'From your mother,' he said.

That night, Emma couldn't sleep. She was stifled in bed with the quilt over her, too chilled with it kicked off. She tried hanging an arm and a leg out at a time, but the localised climate of the air-con frosted her skin. She had to huddle back under the blanket until she was too clammy and uncomfortable to breathe. She felt she had a cold coming. But this house had a way of making you feel like that. There was an electric pepperyness to the air that stuck up your nose and clogged your throat. Great icy blasts were always striking through the ceilings at you. An igloo couldn't have been more draughty.

Emma couldn't sleep. She couldn't get comfortable. She couldn't think of anything but Rob. Rob and that telephone call Emma's mother had made to Rob's father.

Emma was angry about it, a lot angrier than she showed Rob. She pretended to laugh first of all, as if *that* could possibly have stopped her from going to Mallory's with him. But it soon became apparent that Rob wasn't going to take her because his father had made him promise not to. So he wouldn't!

Emma was really cross about it, smiling at Rob through gritted teeth. She couldn't believe he was going to let them tell him what to do. But he was so nice, so very nice. Emma couldn't stay mad at him. He was so good-looking, he could do anything, absolutely anything . . .

o o o

When they got off the train, he ran and leant into someone's front garden and came back with a rose he'd picked for her. A yellow rose, with his blood on its stem where a thorn had pricked him.

He gave her the rose. Then he squeezed so much blood from the end of his fingertip, Emma felt quite like crying. It was the loveliest thing anyone had ever done for her. The way he bled, the red of his blood, the vivid yellow of the rose flower. Emma could have wept. She felt her utmost happiness in those few brief moments.

Rob looked so good, so – it still had to be said, beautiful. Look at him, smiling, laughing, his finger bleeding so beautifully.

It all so easily made up for how ordinary and stupid Emma had begun to feel on the train. She felt so foolish in her New York designer jeans. She looked good in them, but not in the underground at the end of the rush hour with Rob taking her home early because her mother had said so. The underground smelled of after-work armpits and hot feet and Emma's disappointment.

But none of that mattered when Robbie leaned into one of the front gardens on the way from the station and presented Emma with the prize of a bloodied rose bloom. She felt – how did it feel to be in love with someone? How could you tell? Did it feel like, for instance, this? Her heart gave such a leap. She could only laugh and accept the prize and breathe its perfume and laugh again as he bled for her.

o o o

. . . Now she couldn't sleep. She couldn't think of anything but Rob. Unless it was of yellow roses with red, dripping stems. Red, red dripping stems. Or perhaps that was a nightmare that came as soon as she dozed, she couldn't be sure. The stems dripped in her restive night-time waking, bleeding cut roses with all life running from them. She awoke startled, with an image of an enraged Claire Thomas cutting stems with a pair of dreadfully glinting scissors.

She had to get up, put on some clothes. As she passed by her grandmother's room, old Mrs Green called out. Emma ignored her.

She went into the kitchen. There were so many contraptions, banks and banks of white goods and cookers, liquidisers, de-liquidisers, electric knives, electric forks and spoons, heaters, coolers, suckers, blowers, pepper and coffee grinders, salt and wine cellars, such a multitude of buttons and blinking LED indicators it was difficult to locate something as simple as a kettle or an ordinary fridge. When Emma did find some milk, it was so over-chilled she found herself sucking on icy slivers of cream that splintered across her tongue. She was so cold she had a pair of jeans and a winter jumper that she'd borrowed from her mother to brave the inclement indoor weather.

It was the middle of the night. The swimming-pool and grounds outside were spot lit in a blaze of orange light like a false and dirty daytime, with no night allowed. Emma went outside, astonished to find how warm it was. She had to turn back and toss the winter woollies into the kitchen. The summer night was barely any cooler than the day.

Emma touched the water of the pool. She loved the pool more than anything in the whole house and grounds. In fact, looking back at the modern mansion, she felt a kind of foreboding of malevolence, or some kind of a threat.

But the pool was gorgeous. Its very simplicity welcomed her in this hot and humid summer. Even here, in the middle of the night, Emma could have slipped into its calm water and swam, cooled and supported, reassured that hers was the right and only way.

She glanced at the house. She had doubts: massive, but ill-defined gaps in her self-confidence. Looking back at the imposition of what was now her home, Emma could feel the insecurity of having to rely on herself. It was as if she wasn't up to her new status, as if she could fail badly at it.

Then she remembered yesterday afternoon with Rob. With him, there was no doubt. He made her feel so different about herself. This had to mean she was – it *had* to mean she was in love! She had to be in love with Rob, if she felt like this, didn't she?

o o o

In England, it's said, all four seasons can happen in a single day.

All four seasons were happening simultaneously in Emma's bedroom next day. She couldn't get up, but couldn't sleep properly. She heard a click from somewhere, then a climate change would suddenly occur. The film of frost she could have sworn was forming over her quilt disappeared as rain forest steam rose like a fog from the permanently open air vents.

Emma turned over. She was having dreams without remembering what they were about. But the sense of threat they brought stayed with her into consciousness. She had the feeling of a troubled conscience without knowing quite what it was she was supposed to feel guilty about.

From somewhere in the house came the sound of several vacuum cleaners in symphony. The washing-machines were all in action and the driers tumbling like dice clattered through the metal skeleton of the house.

The sun outside was high and hot. Emma turned to look at the blue of the sky to assure herself that every other five minutes winter wasn't alternating with this long hot summer. As she turned, she saw a face at the window peering in at her. She let out a little shriek, disappearing under her quilt. When she reappeared, the face had gone. Then a soapy sponge smeared the window with suds. Emma jumped out of bed, heading for the loo in her Jacuzzi room. She slid open the vast table of a door that allowed access to her walk-through wardrobe. She halted. A strange, prickly feeling shivered across her skin. It felt almost like fear, so strange it was to see the jacket she'd dumped in the High Street after dancing in Mallory's that night.

Behind her, the rubber blade of the window-cleaner's hand window-wiper squeaked over the glass. Emma glanced round at it. The man's face appeared momentarily again. She looked back into the wardrobe, half expecting the jacket to have disappeared, like some kind of ghostly apparition. But there it hung, cleaned and pressed and looking not so much as even shop-soiled. It was hanging right in the middle, exactly before her as she stood there with the sliding door open and the window-cleaner's squeegee squeaking behind her.

She stepped in, carefully moving round the garment as if it meant her harm. It didn't move, but hung there too new, suggesting that Mallory's hadn't happened. Or at least, shouldn't have.

For all the jacket suggested, Emma's feelings for Rob altered nothing. Emma couldn't do a thing.

○ ○ ○

There was a brace of window-cleaners washing down the house from different sides. Emma could sense, as she shivered her way down the stairs, the smell of fresh paint coming from somewhere. From outside, through an open doorway, Emma could hear a cement mixer turning. An electrician failed to notice her pass by as he dragged a swollen belly of coloured wires from a hidden duct.

'What's happening?' she said, as her mother appeared from one of the blast furnaces in the kitchen.

'Nothing,' she said, accidentally stepping into a greased baking tray.

Emma noticed her grandmother perched on the edge of a huge mug of tea as Violet seemed to glide by on wheels for some four or five yards.

'I'm cooking a turkey', Violet said, stepping out of the tray, 'for the weekend.'

'There are people all over the house,' Emma said, feeling the way her mother and grandmother were looking at her.

'I have to – someone has to make sure things get done,' her mother said.

'Someone has to,' her grandmother's voice echoed across the kitchen from the deep well of her tea mug.

'Because the heating has to be sorted,' her mother said.

'The heating does,' her grandmother shivered.

'And the upstairs wants redecorating,' her mother this time.

'Redecorating? Why does it?'

'Because I need to feel,' her mother started to say. She stopped, almost stammering for words. 'Because I don't like it like that,' she said, in the end. Emma looked away from her mother to her grandmother. She too was watching Violet. Emma looked back. Her mother looked so confused, so very nearly afraid. 'All sorts of things need attention,' her mother said.

Emma looked at her. So did her grandmother. 'Are you all right, Vi?' Emma's grandmother said.

'Things need cleaning,' her mother said, staring at her. 'Cleaning and pressing. Like expensive jackets, when the police start bringing them back in such a disgusting state.'

They stood there, saying nothing, looking, that was all, while all around them workmen were pulling bits off the house and putting them back together in a different way.

'And why are you up so late?' Emma's mother said, with her hand suddenly disappearing into the rear end of a huge turkey.

'She's up all hours, Vi,' her grandmother said. 'I've heard her, moving about.'

'Is that true, Emma? Can't you sleep? Emma? Where are you going?'

'To have a shower.'

'Have your breakfast. Emma! Have your breakfast.'

'Mum, I don't like the toast. I'm fine. I'll get something out.'

'Are you going out? Where are you going? Emma, please listen to me. Emma! Please – are you listening to me? Emma?'

'She's not listening to you, Vi,' old Mrs Green said, as Emma left the kitchen.

'No, I know, Mum,' Violet was saying as Emma came back in.

'No,' Emma said, 'I'm not listening. And I won't listen until you start talking to me and stop making phone calls about me to people you don't know and talking to them about things you don't understand!'

As she walked away, Emma could feel the shocked silence in the kitchen even through all the clatter and crash of the technicians trying to sort out the destructive atmosphere reverberating through this hot and cold, uncomfortable house.

o o o

The police had brought back her jacket. It seemed she couldn't go out, couldn't move without everyone knowing where she was and what she was doing.

All the way up the High Street she could see the glances directed at her. The glances were looking for sneak previews of some kind of interesting behaviour or the other. They made her feel as if they were expecting something of her, these people she did or didn't know, who knew her; people she had known, but now couldn't trust not to glance at her as if she was someone else.

A group of girls she barely knew from school passed a comment between them. Emma had to walk past as they all tried not to laugh. Or at least pretend to be trying not to laugh.

She wasn't like them any more; Emma knew that. She'd wanted it that way. But they were so hostile about it. Emma could have cut unspoken comments from the hot air as she went by. The group of girls burst into laughter the second she passed. They knew nothing about her, as far as she knew. Yet there was enough to go on to make them all laugh. Women her mother's age and older were looking at her as if she already had a reputation of some kind. They recognised her, one after the other, then turned away. Emma thought that they were intimidated by money, but felt personally slighted. It made her feel that she wanted to move away, far away from here.

She heard laughter from behind her. Looking back, there was that bunch of girls from school. One of them flicked a cigarette butt in Emma's direction. Emma walked on, quickly. She knew these girls. She and Helen had never liked them. Some of them were friends with Claire Thomas.

Emma could hear the comments coming from behind her. She walked quickly towards the Italian café. She had been hungry, but the hunger had gone away. Her mouth was dry.

'Greenback!' some of the girls were calling out. 'Oi, Greenback. Show us your money.' Emma felt like running. She couldn't do it. They'd never let her get away. She almost stopped and turned to face the little crowd. There must have been seven or eight of them, too many for Emma to confront.

She felt quite afraid.

The Italian café was a long way up the road yet. People were passing. They must have seen that the girls were intimidating Emma. Emma knew that they must have seen. They simply chose to do nothing about it.

Emma's breathing was quickening. These girls were sometimes in trouble for fighting at school, that's on the days they even bothered to turn up. Or when they were there they were hanging round in a bunch smoking and spitting and acting like a gang of thick boys. They'd never liked Emma or Helen,

Helen especially for some reason. Helen always said it was Claire's doing. She had to keep right out of their way.

Emma had always been tarred with Helen's brush. Now Helen was going shopping with Claire, and Emma had something over and above everything they'd ever have, the lot of them.

They were jealous. They were also spiteful. Emma could hear their spiteful remarks from behind her as she hurried up the High Street. From the sound of their voices, they were getting much closer. Nobody took any notice. Emma felt alone on the busy street in the late morning sun. This wasn't right. It just wasn't right. They shouldn't be allowed to treat her like this.

She saw an old neighbour from where they used to live coming out of one of the shops. Another of the girls' cigarette ends flicked by Emma on the pavement.

'Mrs Watts,' Emma called. Mrs Watts halted, looking up. Emma got to her just as the girls were about to catch her up. Mrs Watts had that same strange, almost reluctant look on her face as Emma approached.

'Hello, Emma,' she said.

'Mrs Watts,' Emma said again, too loudly, as the girls passed left and right of them on the pavement. Mrs Watts was glancing at them as they passed. 'It's lovely to see you again, Mrs Watts,' Emma was saying, but really meaning it. Mrs Watts looked embarrassed. As far as Emma could remember, she'd never had a conversation with Mrs Watts without her mother being there. She looked as if somebody had died and she was struggling to find something sympathetic to say.

'Yes,' she said, 'how are you, Emma?'

'Oh,' Emma said, 'fine. How are you?'

The girls had passed by. Emma could see that they'd lost their impetus, that they'd look stupid standing there while Emma had a chat with some woman. They disappeared into one of the clothes shops.

'And how's your mother?' Mrs Watts was saying to Emma. 'She's in Spain I hear, isn't she?'

'No,' Emma said. 'She's at home. My dad's gone to Spain.'

'Ah,' Mrs Watts said. Emma could see a look coming into her face. 'Ah. Your father's in Spain, but your mother's stayed at home.' The other girls had disappeared into that shop. Emma was left with Mrs Watts on the pavement. Mrs Watts was looking at Emma with another kind of expression on her face.

'Yes,' Emma found herself saying, 'he's gone with a friend.'

'Ah,' Mrs Watts said again. 'A friend, eh?' she said, almost smiling, but not quite. Almost, but not quite.

∘ ∘ ∘

They came back. As soon as they saw Emma pass by the clothes shop, the gang of girls came back out. They were shouting things at her. She practically ran up to the Italian café. Robbie was serving at the counter.

'Emma,' he said, in a lowered voice, 'what are you doing here?' They were the only ones in the café. Rob was looking about nervously.

'They're following me,' Emma said, wanting to look afraid for Rob. She *was* afraid. She wanted him to want to help her.

'My dad doesn't like my friends hanging round the café,' he said. Emma halted. It was as if he wanted her to simply leave, with that little lot outside waiting for her. Then one of them banged on the window.

'Oh no!' Rob said. 'Go and sit down. I'll bring you a coffee.' Emma sat at one of the tables. She could hear the door opening and closing at the other end of the café. Her back was towards the counter and the door.

'Greenbacks!' some of the girls were calling in through the open door.

'What's going on?' Emma heard Rob's father saying.

'I don't know,' Rob said. He was making Emma's coffee.

'Who's that for?' Emma heard Mr Britto saying. She felt Rob pointing her out. Another bang came, shaking the glass front of the café. The girls outside were pushing each other into it.

'Hey!' Mr Britto was calling. Emma could hear him walking across the floor tiles to the door. Rob appeared at her table with the coffee.

'I had to see you,' Emma whispered.

Over by the door, Mr Britto was speaking to the gang of girls outside. 'What do you want?' he was saying.

'Some ice-cream,' Emma heard one of them say.

'I have to work,' Rob said to Emma, 'you know that. You can't come here like this.'

'No ice-cream for you,' Mr Britto was saying. 'Go away now. I don't want you here.'

'Our friend's in there,' another girl was saying.

'I need to see you,' Emma whispered, looking up at Rob.

'Your friend?' Mr Britto said. 'Who's your friend?'

'She is!' they said. 'Emma! We're here. Emma! Come on.' The door was closed on them. Emma was looking up at Rob. His dad was coming towards them.

'Dad,' Rob said quickly, 'this is Emma. Emma Green, you know?' Emma looked up at Mr Britto. He looked a lot like Rob, only bald.

'Why do you bring these girls down here?' Mr Britto said to Emma.

'I didn't,' she said. 'They're following me. They're not my friends.'

'You know them, Rob?' his dad asked him. Emma watched him nodding. He looked very serious, as if he was in an awful lot of trouble.

'Get rid of them,' Mr Britto said. 'Then get this one a cab home. You promised me you wouldn't be seeing this one.'

'I didn't –' Rob tried to say.

'Get this one a cab!' Mr Britto almost shouted. He walked away, shaking his head. 'You think I don't have trouble enough, without phone calls from mothers? Eh? You think I don't have trouble enough? I don't see any customers. All I see is trouble-makers.'

'I'm sorry,' Rob whispered to Emma. 'I'll have to call you a cab. I'm sorry.' Emma could hear Rob's father shifting cups and glasses so roughly she wondered why they didn't break. 'I'll call you,' Rob whispered. 'I'll call you. Don't give up on me.' Emma watched him walking away under the angry eye of his father. She felt for him and for herself. They were together in this. They were.

Mr Britto was an ogre.

He didn't call.

He didn't call.

He didn't call.

Days. Days. Emma slept badly. She couldn't go out. There was nowhere to go. She quarrelled with her mother.

Emma's mother also didn't go out. There was something wrong. Emma remembered the look on Mrs Watts' face in town the other day. She realised now that same look crept over faces wherever she went. Her mother must have suffered from it.

Her father didn't call. Emma bickered, turning on her mother, on her grandmother.

Rob didn't call. Nobody did. Emma left it, left it. A week. More. Days. She couldn't sleep. 'Don't give up on me,' Rob had said.

Eventually, one evening, quite late, she had to pick up that telephone receiver. It rang, twice, three times, four, five.

Then, 'Hello?' Rob's father.

'Is Rob there?'

'No. Who's calling?'

'This is Emma.'

A silence. 'No, he's not here.'

'Would you tell him I called?'

'Yes, I'll tell him.'

The line went dead, cutting off that man's ogrous voice. How Emma hated him. He was a tyrant, treating people like that. Rob must hate him.

o o o

Still he didn't call. Days went by. They were so hot. The nights were too, outside the house. Emma walked into town in the dead of night. Night after dead night she walked there to stand opposite the Italian café and think of Rob in his bed.

She tried to see him on Friday afternoon, but he had to stay in the café. Emma watched him from the bookshop opposite. He worked all afternoon. Emma had to go home to sleep. She was dizzy with tiredness. But late that evening, very late, after Rob's gig in Mallory's, she tried the phone again. Her mother had been watching her all evening, trying to make sure Emma wasn't going out. Emma was watched, all the time, wherever she went. Home, out, it didn't matter. Late that Friday evening, with everyone else in bed, Emma tried the phone again. It rang only once.

'Hello?' It was Rob's hushed voice.

'It's me,' she whispered.

'Emma,' he whispered back. 'Oh, Emma, it's you.'

'Yes,' she said.

'Oh, it's so – listen,' he whispered, 'it's really great to speak to you. I've been – you know, all the time. We've got no one to help in the café. It's driving me –'

'Why haven't you called me?'

'Emma, I'm sorry. It's driving me insane. I'm working, all the time. It's him. You've seen what he's like.'

'Yes, I have.'

'Yes. I'm sorry, Emma. Don't go away. I need, you know – one day I'm going to get free of it all. I tell you –'

'Why do you do it then?'

'What? I have to. Listen, I think he's coming. I've got to go. I'll call you. I'm missing you like mad.'

Emma let him go. She smiled. She laughed. He was missing her like mad. Rob was missing her. She was happy. Oh, so, so happy. Then she was happier still when the telephone went and he was back.

'It's all right,' he whispered, 'he's gone to bed. Emma, have you missed me?'

Emma thought she was going to faint. 'I can't tell you,' she said. 'Rob, why do you let him –'

'Don't. Emma, please don't. I'm dying to get away. One day, I promise.'

'And me,' Emma said. 'Soon. Away, as far as possible. America – what do you say?'

'Yeah,' she heard Rob say, 'perfect. America. I'd love to.'

'Why don't we?' Emma said.

'Yeah,' said Rob, 'why don't we?'

'When can I see you?' Emma said.

'Soon,' he said. 'Just let me get things sorted. Okay? Emma? Okay?'

'Okay,' she said. 'Okay.'

o o o

She tried to sleep, but couldn't. She had to walk back to town, stand watching his bedroom window from the other side of the street. She walked back home. It was nearly morning by the time she got back. She went to bed exhausted.

During the day the technicians went at the house with drill and hacksaw and roaring blowtorch. A hand-grinder screeched through Emma's morning sleep, its burnt fragments spitting like the sparks of Emma's hot dreams.

Every night she walked to town to look up at Rob's room. Every day she went to the bookshop to look across the road to the Italian café. She kept imagining seeing Claire there before her waiting for Rob in the street. The image was going to drive her crazy.

The sun shone on to the road between the bookshop and the Italian café. Emma refocused through the glass of the bookshop, through the sunshine, through the glass of the café, on to nothing. She couldn't see him.

Her mother had been on at her for getting up so late. 'What's wrong with you?' she had said, as Emma was eating her breakfast at lunchtime. 'What's wrong with you?'

'She's up all hours,' Emma's grandmother was saying. 'I've heard her, moving about late at night.'

'Is that true Emma?' her mother said, looking closely at her. 'Can't you sleep?'

'I'm all right,' Emma said. 'I'm all right. Leave me alone.'

I'm all right, she was trying to tell herself, focusing through the sunlit glass on to nothing in the low lighting of the Italian café. She wanted to see Rob, that was all. She wanted to talk to him again, to laugh with him. She wanted to touch him to be sure that he was real.

Nothing else felt real.

Something was going wrong inside her, to make her feel like this. She was afraid of too much. She was afraid of missing out on too much. Rob had said he would go with her to America. She imagined the two of them, together, in New York.

Emma waited for him in the bookshop until he appeared in jeans and tee-shirt on the street. Emma looked left and right for any signs of Claire Thomas.

Rob looked great. Every time she saw him she fell for him more and more. She watched him start off up the road, walking towards the park. Emma set off after him, calling to him as soon as they were a safe enough distance from the café. Emma called to him. He turned. He smiled. Oh, yes! He smiled. He was pleased to see her.

'What are you doing here?' he said, as Emma ran to him. He put out his hand.

Emma took it. She took his hand. 'I'm just – you know,' she said, laughing. 'Are you going to the park?'

Rob smiled. They went to the park together. 'It's good to see you, here, unexpectedly like this,' he said.

Emma smiled. She didn't know what to say. The sun was very hot, so they walked in the shade of the horse chestnut trees. 'I've missed you,' Emma said, spontaneously.

Rob stopped. 'Have you?' he said, turning to face her. He looked into her face, into her eyes.

She was looking back into his, deep, deep into his. 'Yes,' she said, softly. 'I've missed you so much.'

For a moment, Rob seemed to concentrate on her hairline. Then on her chin. He looked at her whole face bit by bit, taking in every detail. Emma had never, ever been looked at, been looked into, so closely. It was disconcerting, unnerving, wonderfully exciting. Her heart was beating so hard and fast she could hear it.

His mouth, when he kissed her, was warm, soft, perfect. This was perfect, the day, the park, Robbie Britto. Emma was certain now. She was all right. Now she could be confident. She was in love with him. 'I have to see you tonight,' she whispered. She had made up her mind, once and for all. Rob was so much a part of where she was going, what she was going to be, there was no longer any question.

He kissed her beautifully under the horse chestnut trees out of the sunlight. Emma felt in his kiss that he loved her at least as much as she him. There was no longer any question. She was going to give him . . . everything.

'I have to see you tonight,' she whispered as he held her.

He was silent a long, long time. Emma could feel the loaded significance in his silence. This is it, she was thinking, this, is absolute. For both of us.

She waited, shivering with the thrill of the anticipation of his voice. A slight, magical breeze whispered through the five-fingered leaves above them. Emma stood in Rob's arms, listening to the rustle of the leaves, waiting for him to speak, to give his answer to her.

'I have to go over to Fidge's,' he finally said. Emma felt his hold loosening, preparing to let her go again. 'I have to go over to Fidge's. He's got some new tunes.' He looked at her, smiling. 'I can't tell you how much I love it when Fidge gets us some new tunes,' he said.

Two

'**M**ind your own business!'

'It is my business! Where have you been?'

'What does it matter where I've been? Nowhere. I haven't been anywhere. To town. Surely I can go to town?'

'I know you've been to town. You were seen.'

'Oh! Oh, it's like that, is it? You've got your spies out again, have you?'

'Never mind about that. It doesn't matter how I know what I know, just that I know what I know and what I know is –'

'What? What *are* you talking about?'

'Listen to me!'

'I think you *should* listen, Emma,' her grandmother was saying.

'You were in the park,' Emma's mother went on, 'you were seen in the park. You thought you weren't, but you were.'

'I don't care.'

'Emma,' the old lady was saying from the other side of the room, 'don't say you don't care.'

'But she doesn't care, Mum,' Emma's mother said.

'Don't talk about me as if I wasn't here,' Emma cried, wanting, really, to feel the comfort of her grandmother's birdlike grip round her wrist. If only they wouldn't keep doing this to her, treating her in this way. 'Why must you always –'

'Emma! My daughter, doing that in the park!'

'What? – Doing what?'

'You know what.'

'What? What was I doing? You tell me.'

'Tell her Vi.'

'Be quiet, Mum.'

'I wish both of you would be quiet,' Emma was saying.

'Well we won't,' her mum said. 'I won't be quiet, not while my daughter, who's still at school, goes round snogging boys in the park and –'

'What? Rob kissed me. That's all. He kissed me.'

'Yes! In full view of – in full view! – Emma, what's happening to you?'

'Nothing! Nothing. I'm not doing anything wrong, Mum.'

'That's your opinion,' Emma's grandmother said. She was weighed down under what looked like a polar bear, but happened to be a white fur rug, under which an electric blanket glowed like a nuclear reactor.

'Nan,' Emma said, 'you don't understand.'

'No,' her Nan agreed, 'I don't.'

'I'm not doing anything anyone my age doesn't do.'

'Yes you are,' Emma's mother said, picking up a new dish cloth. 'You're dancing in pubs all of a sudden, on your own, too – No!' she snapped, as Emma opened her mouth to speak.

Emma watched her wiping the work surfaces. Violet was practically sprinting the length of the kitchen and back. Emma was watching her mother as she began to disappear into the kitchen distances. At the other end, she turned and ran with ammonia spray and cleaning cloth back to the starting line. Violet was puffing by the time she made it back. She looked down the long length of the worktop as if to gauge how far she'd come and in what time.

'No!' she snapped, coming abruptly to a halt. 'You are different from other people your age, because you're different to what you were, which was right, for your age. Now you're not. You're wrong.'

∘ ∘ ∘

'I'm not wrong,' Emma was saying to herself. 'She's wrong. *They're* wrong. All of them. They don't understand.' She was waiting for Rob's lunchtime to come round again. The street was a river of powerful sunlight against the throb and ache of Emma's eyes.

She preferred the street at night. Being lonely was easier on your own than when pressed and persecuted by the stares of strangers. Any one of these people could be one of her mother's informers. Violet seemed to know her every move, as if a private eye were following her everywhere.

Emma refocused her own private eyes on to the darkness inside the cool of the Italian café. So far she hadn't managed to spot Rob at all. Not once. She was hot in the bookshop and the charity shop opposite the café, sweating over Rob's appearance.

Where was he? It was getting so late.

Her mother had told her she had to be back inside a couple of hours. She didn't want her daughter kissing boys in full view of – of whom, exactly, Emma had not been able to discover. Her mother was reluctant to say. But Emma had been watched. Whatever she did, she was watched.

'Of course you are,' Violet said. 'Of course you're watched. Don't you understand what people are like?'

Yes, Emma understood what people were like. They were jealous. They wanted it to go wrong for her. It was horrible, this little town with all its prying eyes. She had to get away. She *had* to.

'Come with me,' she'd said to Rob. 'Come with me to America, to New York – Rob, come with me to the only place in the world. I can't tell you what it'll be like. I know movie stars, right, Tom and Angelica Banks, and they can get us –'

But what happened?

'Emma! I have to work. My father needs me at the moment.'

Emma needed him. She *needed* him. He didn't seem to understand the depth of her feeling. His father couldn't possibly have needed him to this extent. Emma was shrivelling, drying up in the heat of the English summer in book-shops and High Street charity shops, trying not to get noticed.

Look how she needed him, how she waited hours for him to appear. And he didn't. He wasn't there. She couldn't see him. She could see his father there on his own. She couldn't see Rob. He wasn't there.

She waited for hours, going out of her mind. Bookshop. Charity shop. Going out of her mind. Rob wasn't there.

But Claire was.

Claire Thomas came walking up the street as if she was allowed by Rob's father to hang out in the Italian café. Emma wasn't allowed near the place. Rob said his father wouldn't have it. Yet when Claire Thomas came floating up the street, she was able to push open the glass door as if it was what she was *supposed* to do. Emma was suddenly all attention, the hairs on the back of her neck standing up in a surprising feeling of fear. She watched Claire open and casually pass through the café door. Emma found herself half-way out of the bookshop door, her eyes fixed across the road before the hand clapped on to her shoulder.

'I've been watching you,' a man's voice said.

And I've been watching everything else, Emma was thinking. Even then she couldn't move her eyes from what might be happening inside the café over the road

'Where do you think you're going with that?' the dislo-cated voice said. Emma, for the first time, looked and saw the face of the man speaking to her. 'What do you think you're doing?' he said, looking into her hands.

Emma looked down to discover that she was holding a book. She opened her mouth to speak but found her focus back on the other side of the road. 'I don't,' she managed to say. Then she said nothing. She could just make out Claire sitting on a stool at the coffee bar.

'You'd better come with me,' the man was saying to her.

But Emma couldn't hear him. Her attention was fixed on the sight of Rob's father coming round the customer side of the coffee bar to sit at a stool and start talking to Claire Thomas.

'I'm sorry,' the man was saying, taking Emma by the arm, leading her back to the shop, 'but I must insist that you come back into the shop with me. Come on,' he was saying, as Emma's fixed attention strained her neck backwards to see what was going on across the sunlit road in the gloom of the Italian café.

o o o

'You were stealing!'

'I wasn't stealing. How can you say that?'

'You were taking that book out without paying for it!'

'I wasn't – I didn't, did I? I paid for it.'

'Yes, only because you were caught. You were caught taking books without paying for them. That's stealing, in my book!'

'What book's that?' Emma's grandmother said. 'What book's that, Vi?'

'What?' Emma's mother said, looking confused. She was up to her armpits in one of the kitchen sinks. The water was filling up her rubber gloves.

'What book's she on about?' Mrs Green said to Emma.

'Anyway,' Violet snapped, turning from the sink, her gloves brimming full of washing-up water, 'you think paying for it makes it all all right, don't you? You think it doesn't matter what you do?'

'I don't,' Emma tried to say.

'Don't answer me back!' her mother almost shouted at her. Emma's grandmother's eyes opened wide in surprise.

'You think,' Violet said, more slowly, 'that it doesn't matter what you do, as long as you can pay your way out of it, don't you!'

'No, I – I don't – it wasn't like that. I wasn't thinking what I was doing. It was an accident.'

'That doesn't make any difference. The man in the shop thought you were stealing a book. Everyone thought you were.'

'Everyone? Who's everyone? Who have you got following me around spying on me? Eh? Who's following me?'

'No one.'

'Well how come you always know exactly what –'

'What did you expect?' Violet said, raising her hands. Soapy water ran out of her gloves. For a moment all three of them looked at the soapy splashes on the tiles of the kitchen floor. Violet looked confused, worrying where the water might have leaked from. A gang of plumbers went at that moment hammering floorboards, trying to locate lost pipes and pumps and immersion heaters that were constantly boiling all the washing water into steam. Violet Green looked up. Emma could see all the confusion and the confused worry in her mother's thinning face.

'What did you expect?' Violet said again. 'Did you really think people round here weren't going to watch everything you do, watch you everywhere you go? Did you really think that wouldn't happen?'

Emma stood looking at her mother, realising how darkly tired she had grown, how much weight she had lost very recently. 'Is that why,' she said, 'you've stopped going out?'

Violet's rubber gloves squeaked under pressure. 'No, I –' she stammered, glancing at Emma's Nan. 'No. I just don't need to go out. People can come here, if they want to see me.'

'Well why don't they then?'

'I don't know. They've changed. I don't know why. All they do is keep calling me. People keep calling me. Do you know why? Do you? They want to keep calling me and telling me about you stealing things and –'

'I haven't stolen anything.'

'No, not yet you haven't. But I have to hear about you

hanging about in town on your own. What's happened to all your friends?'

'What's happened to yours?'

'This isn't about me!'

'You never had any friends, that's why,' Emma said. 'Not proper ones, anyway. Neither did I.'

'Emma! You're making me – Mum!' Violet turned and said to Emma's Nan. 'Did you hear that?'

Emma's Nan's head shot out of her blankets, looking round into all the corners of the room. 'What was it?' she said. 'More water? What was it?'

'No,' Emma's mother said, 'I know what's responsible for this. It's that boy, isn't it?'

'What boy?' old Mrs Green said, looking round for one. 'What boy, Vi?'

'That one in the café. What's his name?'

'I don't know,' Mrs Green said.

'Rob,' said Emma.

'Robert,' said her mum. 'Him. Him, taking you drinking.'

'I wasn't –'

'Robert?' old Mrs Green was saying.

'Taking girls like you into pubs like that. Taking you into the park.'

'Taking me? I took him!'

'There!' Violet said. 'Did you hear that, Mum? Did you hear that?'

'What?' said old Mrs Green. She was still looking everywhere for some evidence of a boy or something like the leaking water that she was supposed to have heard. 'I can't hear anything,' she was saying.

'It's all wrong,' Violet said. The rubber gloves were slipping over her wrists, falling down until she looked as if she had long ape-arms hanging down to her lower thighs. 'It's all wrong,' she said, slapping her long rubber arms on to the worktop, 'my daughter, doing all that. Emma', she said, staring into her daughter's face, 'that isn't you. It isn't you at all.'

'Who is it then?' Emma said.

'I don't know,' her mother said. Her grandmother was shaking her head. She didn't know either. 'But what do I know,' her mother said, 'is that's an end to it. I'm telling you now, I'm not having any daughter of mine hanging about in the High Street with everyone watching, waiting for boys to go stealing books with and kissing in public places and drinking in pubs.'

'Mum, it's not –'

'I don't care!' she shouted, her vehement rubber gloves flying, flinging one off.

'Ooh, Gawd!' old Mrs Green said.

'I don't care! That's an end to it! Do you hear me, Emma? That's it. It's all over!'

o o o

Emma was crying in her room.

They didn't understand. How could they? The only person in the world that might have had a hope of understanding anything at all about what Emma was going through, was away and free of it all. Eddie was in Spain with some business associate or entrepreneur, or more likely some bloke he met in the pub who thought it'd be a gas buying a bar in the Costas somewhere. Eddie had been all for it.

Emma was crying in her room.

Eddie was away, free of all of this. He was starting out on his own, actually out there doing something.

Emma was crying in her room.

Violet hadn't the heart to go off with her husband. Emma knew she was afraid to go out now. She seemed confused and humiliated by everything Eddie loved about having money. And Eddie's mother was ill, growing more and more confused on stronger and stronger doses of medication, but Violet

100

seemed to be using her as an excuse. First Paris, then New York, now Spain. Violet didn't want to go. She wanted the safety of her own four walls, her home; although this place, this house, was neither home nor particularly safe.

Practically anywhere would have been safer than this house at the moment, where great lumps were being hacked off by the army of engineers. Its ugly guts were exposed, huge nasty underbellies of ducts and denuded spinal cords of wires flopped in tangles out of the ceilings. Short circuits sparked, static electricity crackled, fire and burglar alarms rang out at any time of day and night like air raid warnings not to sleep peacefully.

Eddie had quite suddenly departed from all this, but old Mrs Green clicked and clacked, shivering under massive blanketry, while Violet struck out with cleaning cloth and condensed bleach for safety, and Emma cried through it all in her room.

She heard a knock at her door. It was her mother's knock, but softer. The knock was more nervous more frail.

'Go away!' Emma cried out. The frail knocking ceased, immediately. It had been too afraid to insist.

The strange thing was, Emma didn't really want the knock to give in like that. She wanted something more determined from it, if only to let her know there was something stronger than herself at this moment, crying in her room. She held her breath through the resigned silence before turning to face the wall. They didn't understand. How could they? Nobody understood. She was losing out, being brought to nothing by everyone.

The man in the bookshop had thought she'd been trying to steal a book. She had so much money, she could have bought all the books in just about the whole shop. The man couldn't see it. He took her money reluctantly, as if she had insulted him. He eventually allowed her to pay, refusing to accept more than the selling price of the book, refusing to recognise

Emma's disassociation with what was happening. He couldn't see that Emma didn't care. Nobody but Emma could see what it meant to her to have to watch Claire Thomas sitting on the customer side of the coffee bar in the Italian café with Mr Britto, chatting to him as if she belonged there. Even with Robbie away somewhere, mysteriously missing somewhere, Claire still chatting with Rob's father in the café from which Emma was routinely, endlessly, cruelly barred.

Emma cried. She could not move outside this house without the eyes of ex-friends on the street humiliating her, and her mother with still further tales to tell.

But then Emma had recognised her mother's anguished intimidated knock on her bedroom door. She could tell suddenly by the frailty of the knock that the spies were also against her mother, reporting back every perceived misdemeanour as an attack on the family's newfound privilege.

Nothing in her mother's timidity was going to be able to prevent Emma from going to Mallory's this Friday. Nothing here could be powerful enough against the strength of feeling that had propelled Emma up the street following Claire Thomas. Having finally paid off the bookseller, Emma had spotted Claire through the insult of the High Street sunshine. She wasn't sure, she couldn't be sure, but something in Claire's composure, something in the spring in her step had wanted to let Emma know that Claire knew she was there. Emma had been so very careful not to be seen, but the sensation she had felt watching Claire was that Claire was sneering at her.

Emma followed at a distance, watching Claire's sneering steps up the High Street and round the corner where they've got the new burger bar now. Emma went after her. She turned the corner but Claire was not there. She turned back. No Claire.

Emma turned and turned. She felt dizzy, sick, even here in

her room with the tears drying on her face she felt stupid as she remembered Helen and Claire's faces watching her turning and turning in the street on the corner outside the new burger bar.

There they were, the two of them, already sitting at a table with Helen's carton of chips and a coke between them, watching Emma turning like a fool outside. She saw Claire lean across and say something to Helen. They both laughed.

They laughed.

Emma had to go in, she looked and felt like such a fool. She had to go in and go up to the counter and order some chips and a drink of her own. She felt sick and foolish waiting there, with Helen and Claire, her ex-best friend and her ex-best friend's worst enemy, in cold collusion against her.

She had to wait for the chips she didn't want to eat. She had to stand there and wait at the counter in the new burger bar on the corner while Claire made it all too clear, all too loudly, that she, Claire Thomas, had got a job working in the Italian café.

Emma was shaking.

The tears fell again as she lay shaking on her bed.

She had had to turn, to walk out of the burger bar without her chips or her drink, because she felt sick.

She felt sick. Lying on her bed, with the tears running back down her face, she could hear the laughter still at her back. She felt sick and wobbly with it. Nothing her mother could say or do could possibly be stronger than the feelings she now harboured. Her mother and grandmother, the weak and sick, were powerless to stop her.

Nothing could stop her going back to Mallory's this Friday night.

∘ ∘ ∘

'I don't have time. I just do not have time to argue with you. I told you. Where are you going? Emma!' Emma stopped. She had her best New York clothes on. She'd had her hair done again. 'Look at you! Look at your face. What do you think you've done to yourself? What have you done to your face?'

'Nothing.' Emma said.

'Look at you,' her mother said, shaking her head. 'I can hardly recognise you.'

'That's good, then,' Emma said.

Her mother was shaking her head. She looked tired herself, worn down, too painfully thin. 'All that make-up. What are you trying to do to yourself?'

'I'm not trying to do anything. I'm trying to be me, that's all.'

'Look,' her mother said, just before the doorbell rang to the tune of 'Viva Espania'. Emma saw it fling a look of pained irony into her mother's face. She knew they were both reminded of the night they had learned of the lottery win, when they had all thought they were on their way to somewhere better.

Emma saw her mother's surprised and pained face glance round left and right at the supposedly better place now surrounding her.

'That's the doctor,' Violet said to her daughter, looking in pained surprise at the beautiful young woman she hardly recognised dressed in the latest New York designer fashion. 'I don't have time to argue with you. Your Nan's not very well at all.'

The door chimes reverberated through the silence. But Emma's mother still didn't move. She was watching her daughter as her daughter stared back at her. They were both looking through the shattered optimism of the chimes, both wondering what had happened and what was going to happen. But whatever did happen, Emma was not to blame. She'd done nothing that anyone of her age wouldn't have done given her new opportunities and privileges. In fact, she'd done a whole lot less than most.

Why was she still here, for a start?

The door chimes rang again. Emma watched her mother physically flinch. 'You'd better get the door,' she said.

'It'll be the doctor,' her mother said.

'All the more reason to get it then.' Another few moments of after-door-chime silence ran on before Emma's mother turned and walked away. Emma heard her talking to the doctor as they trekked through the chilled, wire-strewn halls towards the stairs. She breathed, relieved that it had been the doctor and not her cab.

Her mother didn't, couldn't, understand. How could she, being wrapped up in her agoraphobia, attempting to clean and care her way into coping with her father's new sunny-Spain lifestyle. The Viva door chimes played once again. Emma leapt up, rushing for the door, another new jacket thrown over her shoulder.

Her mother appeared on the stairs. Emma looked up at her. She looked even thinner against the wide berth of the staircase as it turned the corner for the fourth or fifth time on the way down. Emma halted.

'Where are you going?' her mother said, thin and windswept, still wearing her cleaning clothes from the housing estate. Emma moved towards the huge double doors in the huge hall. Subtropical plants wilted all round her in the frosty air. 'Emma!' Emma's hand was ready for the heavy ornate handle of the door. She halted. She hadn't said anything. There was nothing for her to say. She'd seen through to the heart of her mother's despair. It wasn't her fault. 'Don't, Emma. I told you.'

From outside the house, a car horn was going. Door chimes, car horns. From the past, to the future. One passes into the other. Emma looked up at her mother driven almost insane upon the stairs of the house.

'Emma,' her mother said, 'I can't do this. I'm on my own here. This house,' she said looking confusedly around both left and right. 'Your grandmother's not very well.' Emma clasped the handle of the door. 'Did you hear me?' her mother said, more firmly. 'Your grandmother is really not very well.' Emma faltered. Her mother's face looked as if it was about to break down. Her mother looked as if old Mrs Green really was very ill.

But Emma couldn't look back now. The old girl was always getting sick, with one thing or the other. She was old. That's what old people did. They sat in the chair and waited for you, they cared about you without doing anything at all for you, and they got ill. None of it was Emma's fault. It wasn't fair.

It simply was not fair, she was thinking, as she opened the door and went out.

o o o

Nobody understood what she was going through. They were all too wrapped up to bother, preferring instead to listen to the spiteful gossip about her.

So people saw her out, so what? They saw the things they saw, that was all. They couldn't see what she felt, could they? Nobody could see it, so how could anybody begin to understand?

She was staring out of the back window of the taxi. As they drove through the long evening shadows, Emma could begin to see herself reflected in the car window. Yes, she looked pretty good. She looked pretty wild. That's what Rob had called her at Helen's party. That's how she wanted to present herself, with her hair done and her make-up carefully applied. Pretty wild.

The car went under the railway bridge on the bend before the traffic lights. Cars were backed up there, waiting for the lights to change. The taxi stopped in the gloom under the bridge. Emma saw herself clearly in the car window, with her hair done and her make-up carefully applied, looking pretty wild. She looked into her own eyes as they stood out unpainted and undisguised, exposing her to herself and to anyone else with eyes like her own to see.

As the car pulled away, she tried to shrug off the image staring back at her with the unwanted humiliation carried from the burger bar on the corner in the centre of town.

'Off out for the evening, are you?' Emma suddenly heard the cab driver saying. He was looking at her anguished face in the rear-view mirror.

Emma shrugged, her wild and pretty hair flowing, presenting to the cabbie and to the outside world the visage of someone prepared to dance on her own in a bar full of jealous onlookers.

'Mallory's, eh?' the cabbie said, glancing at her. Emma steeled herself against the reflection of his eyes in the mirror. 'Expect you'll be off to some club somewhere afterwards, will you?' he said.

Emma nodded. 'I expect so,' she said. She could hear the lack of conviction in her voice and so decided to overcome it. 'I expect we'll be clubbing in London later on,' she said, too loudly.

The reflected eyes smiled. 'Too right,' he said. 'I would too, if I had your kind of money.'

Emma nodded in the back. Nobody has our kind of money, she was thinking. Ours seems to be a strange, solitary kind of money that nobody can earn or inherit. Our kind of money comes at you like an infection. Emma could still see her mother standing on the too-clean stairs, infected by extreme wealth.

'Yeah,' the cab driver went on, 'it must be really something, all that money, eh?' Emma nodded, she had been about to ask if he knew who she was, but they all knew. There were eyes out, everywhere, knowing full well. 'What's it like then?' he said, glancing back over his shoulder at her. They were going along the High Street now, with the shops all shut and the low sun leering up the street. 'Eh? What's it like, all that money?'

Emma looked out of the window. The Italian café slid by outside. The money infection prickled in her nose and eyes, a tearful, emotional illness. 'It's like,' she started to say.

But what was it like?

'It's like – you know what it's like not having any money, don't you?' she said.

'I know that all right,' he said. 'But it's not like that, is it.'

'No,' she said, 'it's not like that.' It's worse, she was thinking, much worse.

'Must be great,' the cabbie said, indicating to pull over in front of Mallory's Dance Bar. 'Must be really great.'

'No!' Emma screamed.

'Blimey!' he said, ducking. 'Blimey!'

'Go on!' she cried. 'Drive on!'

'But there's –'

'I know,' Emma said. There was Mallory's, sailing by in the other direction. Emma knew. She could see the place. She could also see, approaching the double entry doors to Mallory's, she could see two girls dressed to go out for the evening. They'd both had their hair done. They'd both applied their make-up carefully. They both looked – they were looking pretty wild.

Emma could see them, Helen and Claire, dressed as if they had some money and half a life between them, hair done, make-up and best clothes on, making their way to Mallory's.

'Stop!' Emma shrieked.

'Blimey!' the man said stepping on his brakes. A car behind them had to pull up too quickly, honking his horn. 'What's the matter?' the driver said, turning to look at Emma in the back seat. She was turning back to look behind, watching her ex-best friend and her ex-best friend's ex-worst enemy entering the dance bar before her. 'Are you all right?' Emma could hear the cabbie saying.

'Yes,' she said. 'Wait a minute, please. I'm all right. Just wait a minute.'

She was all right. Everything was. There go Helen and Claire looking like that into Mallory's before her, here she was stuck in a cab outside, Rob was taking days away from work in the café without telling her, and Claire had got herself a job there, in the Italian café. With Rob.

Of course she was all right. She was just waiting outside Mallory's in the cab for Helen to get thrown out for being too young, or too geeky or something. Anything!

'What do you want me to do, love?' the taxi driver said.

'Just stay where you are a minute,' Emma said. 'I'll pay you, don't worry.' Her head was still turned, her eyes still fixed upon the closed doors of Mallory's Dance Bar. She watched while another couple went in. She was trying desperately to breathe. Her mother couldn't bring herself to leave the house any more. The whole world was against her, watching, waiting. Emma's mother stayed at home, burrowing like a grub away from the cruel opinions and the animosity they could all feel on every side.

Emma could feel it. Out there, nobody wanted her to succeed. They were all so spitefully jealous.

Emma hated them, all of them. She didn't belong here. Neither did Rob. They were better than this. Her father had always said so. Emma had to make them admit it.

This was a competition. There were winners and losers, nothing in between.

'I'll have to hurry you, love,' the cabbie said, looking at his watch.

'Turn the car round,' Emma said. 'Take me back up the High Street. You know the Italian café?' The cabbie nodded. 'Take me there,' Emma said.

o o o

The heels of Emma's Italian shoes clacked across the tiles of the floor. Mr Britto was behind the counter on his own. There were only a couple of customers, two young girls dipping into a shared pink ice-cream with two spoons. Rob's father looked up as Emma clacked her way across the tiles to take a stool at the coffee bar. Watching her closely, he didn't look at all surprised to see her. He looked tired. Emma's heart was racing. Her head was swimming. She could feel her own pulse, could have counted it just sitting there, if she could have counted that fast.

Mr Britto sighed deeply. 'What do you want here?' he said. He was looking hard at Emma. She could see Robbie in his eyes. Mr Britto allowed Emma to settle on the stool at the coffee bar.

Emma asked for a cappuccino. He nodded. He was quite bald, with dark hair left only at the back and sides. But he was one of those men that managed to look pretty good in their baldness. He still looked handsome. He still looked a lot like Rob.

Emma tried to breathe more easily. Which wasn't easy. She didn't know what to say now that she was actually facing Robbie Britto's dad. She was on her own with the ogre. He looked calm and purposeful as he made the coffee. She felt ordinary and unconfident as he placed the cup in front of her, sprinkling the frothy surface with chocolate powder.

'Anything else?' he asked her, looking with a determined purpose into her face.

'No,' she said, quietly. 'That's all, thanks. How much is that?'

'That's okay,' he said, holding up his hand, 'it's on me.'

'Oh,' Emma said. 'Oh, thanks.' She stirred in some brown sugar. All the while, Mr Britto was watching her intently.

'You like my coffee?' he said, having watched her sip it.

She nodded. 'Yes, very much.' A pause. His eyes were fixed upon her. Emma's were shifting, avoiding him. She fidgeted on the stool in front of him.

'Robbie's told me,' he said, after an extremely uncomfortable and long silence, 'all about you.'

110

'Oh,' she smiled, 'all good, I hope?' He smiled, too. But briefly. Too briefly to be all good. He had, written there in his tiny pinched smile, a disapproval of her. She knew it. 'I don't think you like me,' she said, feeling her whole face draining of colour.

'I don't dislike you,' he smiled. 'It isn't you.'

Emma was staring, white-faced, into his smile. She could feel his disapproval of her. She felt it as a trembling rage within, a prickly and bristling anger over the surface of her skin. 'I really do think you don't like me,' she said. It was as honest a statement as she could make. Emma felt she had the truth on her side.

Mr Britto's smile disappeared. 'I said I don't dislike you,' he said. There came a long, long pause. He was looking at her, looking at her, before he said, 'Have you come here for a reason?'

Emma faltered. 'I'd like,' she said swallowing, her heart racing still faster, 'I'd really like to, make you – make you an offer.'

Mr Britto laughed. 'Make me an offer? What could you possibly offer me?'

'I can offer you, you know, what you need most,' she said.

'And what might that be, then? Money?'

Emma nodded. 'Yes. I can pay for someone else to take Rob's place. I can pay. I know you need somebody.'

Mr Britto was shaking his head. 'Why don't you go home?' he said.

'No, I – you shouldn't try to make me go home. Please listen to me. He's wasting his time. He's a good DJ. Anybody could run round this place. I'll pay for two people, I don't care.'

'I know you don't.'

'No. It's not me that doesn't care. You're the one keeping him here, don't you see that? I could help him.'

'Oh, yes? How? With more money?'

'It goes a long way. How can he go anywhere, being repressed day after day like a –'

'Repressed? You don't understand, girlie. You don't get it at all. He doesn't need me. And he certainly doesn't need you.'

'You don't know. How could you know.'

'Because I know what you obviously do not. Would you like me to tell you what you are obviously in perfect ignorance of?'

'What could *you* possibly tell *me*? How could you even begin to understand?'

They stopped. There was a crushing silence. Emma could feel the eyes of the two girls fixed upon them over their shared ice-cream. She was breathing as if she'd just run three miles. Her head was swimming. She felt pushed into a corner. It wasn't supposed to be like this. He was supposed to be interested in what she had to say. He needed the money, surely, didn't he? But he was smiling once more, sparkling with a renewed confidence, forcing Emma into a confrontation. She started to feel sick. It wasn't supposed to be like this.

'I don't know what he's said to you,' Mr Britto smiled and said, 'but he doesn't need you. He doesn't need me. He's got a job, on the radio. He's going on Central Radio. Away from here, on his own. In two months time. Do you understand? Away from here. Without any help from me, or from you. He's done it. You're right. He is a good DJ.'

Emma felt sick. She was blinking, swallowing. 'I don't – why would he – I don't believe you,' she said. He shrugged. He was still smiling. Emma felt the tension well up in her. Tears clouded her eyes and her vision. 'Why wouldn't he have told me?' He shrugged again. 'I don't believe you! I don't believe you because you – you'd lie to keep him here, keeping him here when he could be – doing things! That's all it is! I don't believe you!'

The coffee cups were rattling, ringing with the strength and level of Emma's elevating voice. She halted, trembling, with her hands quivering by her sides. She had stood up without realising it. She was staring across the counter at Mr Britto. Tears were running down her face.

He was blinking, ever so slowly. 'Why don't you ask him yourself?' he said, turning his head slowly towards the door. Emma turned. She blinked away her tears. Rob was standing there in his best clothes, freshly washed and clean, but clearly looking embarrassed.

Emma looked into his shocked, embarrassed face. She could see, in his face, that it was all true. 'Why didn't you tell me?' she said. 'Why lie?'

The embarrassment in his face deepened. He glanced towards his father. 'Emma. I didn't mean to say – it wasn't supposed to be like –'

'How could you lie to me like that?'

'I didn't. You said it all. I didn't. You led yourself into believing –'

'You could have told me about the job! You could have at least told me that!'

'How could I? Why should I? I only found out myself this week. I wanted to tell everybody tonight, in Mallory's. But you're here, instead.'

Emma looked back at Rob's father. 'You! You wanted this to happen, didn't you! I know you wanted this to happen!'

Mr Britto was shaking his head. 'I didn't want him to see you at all, remember?'

'It's him!' Emma screeched at Rob. 'It's him! Don't you see how he does it? He's manipulating us. That's why he's given Claire Thomas a job here! That's what he does!'

They were all staring at her. Emma suddenly saw herself reflected in the mirrors on the café walls, white and foaming, desperate. She saw herself suddenly as Rob must be seeing her. The black mascara was running down her over made-up face. Her hair had gone limp with the dampness of her sweat.

The two girls were staring at her over their ice-cream.

Rob's father was staring.

They were all staring at her. But none of them could see her. No one could. She was on her own. She found herself dashing the cup of coffee from the counter, smashing it across the floor. One of the girls let out a little shriek.

'Emma!' Rob shouted.

Emma scratched open her bag, took out a handful of banknotes. She threw them on the counter. 'That's for the coffee!' she shrieked at Rob's father. 'Keep the change!' She ran out into the street. She was desperately trying to get away.

The low relentless sun shone into her face as she ran up the road. She could feel the summer's hot malevolence in the street as Claire Thomas and Helen came out of Mallory's and watched her running the length of the High Street and up past the new burger bar on the corner, opposite the record shop.

Emma's grandmother was wrapped in an arctic blanket, complaining of much too much money. 'What's she going to do with herself?' the old lady was croaking away behind her dentures.

'Where have you been, Em?' her mother was asking.

Emma was turning away. 'My name's not M,' she said.

'Emma', her mum said, 'don't – come here. Where are you going? Come here!'

Emma was trying to get away, but she wasn't going anywhere. There was nowhere to go. Nothing to do. Nothing worked, not any more. 'Come here!' her mother was shouting at her. 'Where are you going?'

'She's got too much,' Emma's grandmother's tombstone teeth clicked. 'She got too much, too soon.'

'Things have got to change,' her mother said.

Emma said, 'You're telling me.'

'Yes, I am telling you.'

'She don't know who she is,' the old granny was saying, over and over.

'There are going to be some changes, my girl. You're going to start telling me where you're going every day for a start.'

'What for?'

'What for? I'll tell you what for, shall I?'

'Tell her what for,' the old lady was chipping in like the echo of a ghost that only Emma could hear.

'Tell me what for,' Emma said. 'Do tell me what for, if you can.'

'Oh, I can.'

'Course she can,' the shadow said.

'Then do.'

'To stop you making an even bigger fool of yourself than you already have.'

Emma laughed bitterly. 'Me?'

'Yes, you.' The old shadow was nodding, her head going up as her teeth were on their way down, then head falling as the teeth came rattling up. 'Yes, you. Don't think I haven't heard of your little – your little escapades.'

'Oh yes?' Emma said. The old lady was still nodding. 'Who's been telling tales now then, eh?'

'Never you mind.'

'Never you mind,' came the ghostly echo.

'I do mind. People should mind their own business, that's what –'

'It is their business when I get phone calls about you going round insulting people and breaking things and –'

'I pay, don't I?'

'Oh yes, you pay. That makes it all all right I suppose, does it?' The old lady was shaking her head. Emma was already tired of this. They'd been here so many times already. The whole thing was making her feel sick and stupid and confused. It wasn't anybody's business. They should all learn to keep their big noses out.

'It's too easy, isn't it,' her mother was going on. 'Too easy just to pay. Nothing matters then. Nothing matters, does it? Eh?'

'Of course it matters,' Emma said.

'She's got too much,' her grandmother started to say. 'Girls of her age, they didn't ought to have so much, they didn't.'

'All right, Mum,' Emma's mother said to her. 'Let me deal with this.'

'Deal with this?' Emma said. 'Deal with this? What's to deal with? You think I'm something that needs dealing with, do you? Is that what you think?'

'I think,' her mother said, 'that you're having problems with coping, that's what I think.'

'Well I don't think so,' Emma told her. 'I don't think so at all. It's not me, is it?'

'Who is it then?' her mother asked her, with her grand-mother looking at her, asking the same question with her eyes.

Emma halted. Who was it? Who had done all this to her? 'It's not me, is it,' Emma said to her mother and grand-mother. 'I'm not the one with the problems, am I?'

'Who is it, then?' her mother asked. They were both looking at her. Emma's head was swimming. The pressure inside her was almost unbearable. Nobody could see her. They didn't understand. They just did not understand.

'It's you, isn't it?' she said to the two of them.

'Emma,' her mum's voice said.

Emma was staring back at the two of them in exaspera-tion. 'It's you. You, and you. It's you and you and people like you. I mean, look at this place. Just look at this place.' The old grandmother was looking about at all the flowery fittings and the amassed, nasty ornaments in a forest of petrified figurines. 'Look at her!' Emma was spitting, looking at her grandmother. 'It's all of it. It's nothing, is it? You and her.'

'Emma,' her mum's voice said, full of warning.

'Well look at you. Look at you! What's the matter with you? You can't go out or see anybody or do anything but go round cleaning this place all day long. You're so scared of everybody you can't even move outside these walls. Can you! Answer me! Can you!' She was staring at her mother.

Violet stood pale and trembling, speechless. Emma knew the truth about her. There was nothing she could say. Emma knew the truth about everything and everybody. But nobody knew the first thing about her. Nobody understood what she was going through. It was just too much to bear.

'I'm sick of this place!' she screamed.

'Don't you think I am?' her mother screamed back. 'Don't you think I don't hate this place more than anything?'

'Vi!' Mrs Green was calling. 'Violet! I don't feel –'

'And her!' Emma screamed at her grandmother. 'Her! She's like a –'

'Emma!'

'Violet,' the old lady was trying to say in a failing, weakening voice. 'Violet, I think I'm going to –'

'Emma, nothing! She's like a – like some kind of parrot over your shoulder all the time. The two of you, always getting at me! Going on and on –'

'Emma! That's enough!'

'Violet. I –'

'Enough? I haven't even started. Enough? Look at her. What's the matter with her? She belongs in a home, that's where she belongs!' The old lady's mouth was opening and closing. Emma's mother's mouth opened as if to scream, but no words would come out. 'She's nothing but an old – she's just an old nuisance!' Emma hammered on. 'She's nothing but a liability. Why don't you get rid of her? Eh? Why don't you get rid of her? We can afford it. You don't have to be a cleaning lady any more. Just get rid of all this old rubbish! Just get rid of it all!'

o o o

Emma smashed up the stairs, her cheek and ear ringing with the noise and the pain of having been suddenly slapped.

'Get upstairs!' her mother had shrieked into her face. 'Get upstairs! Now!'

Emma smashed up the stairs. 'And where's my dad!' she was screaming down. 'Where's my dad gone, eh?'

'I don't know where he's gone, do I!' her mother was shrieking back up the stairs at her. 'How should I know where he is? Who am I? Get in your room.'

'Get lost!'

'No! Get in your room. Don't you dare come out till I –'

But Emma was slamming the door of her room, shutting out the noise behind her. She was livid, shaking. She was white, except for the raw red of the handprint across her face. That had been quite a slap. Emma had never been hit by anyone, in the whole of her life. Not by anyone. She looked into the mirror on her dressing-table. The mirror was surrounded by low-level bare electric light bulbs like in an actor's dressing-room. The low lighting illuminated Emma's pale trembling face starkly, showing too graphically where the clap of the hard hand had caught her. Her hurt face was showing there. Her lips were quivering, her eyes blinking back the tears of pain and anger and frustration. She had never been hit by anyone, in her life. Now this. Now that woman had chosen to attack her in this way. It wasn't fair. Emma didn't deserve to be assaulted. She knew it wasn't just what she'd said about her grandmother. It couldn't have been. There was too much force behind it, too much pain and anguish driving her mother on.

No, it had to be because her mother just could not cope. It was as Emma had said. She was suffering from her own inadequacy. Emma knew, she understood. Neither her mother nor her grandmother could keep up. Emma's father was out there. He was living it, as it should be lived: to the full. Grabbing it with both hands, wanting it, taking it.

The rest of them were down here fearing the worst, when out there somewhere, the best awaited them and all the moneyed people like them. It glittered on the horizon, heady with fame and other people's admiration. All you had to do was to reach far enough, to struggle for it hard enough. It was not a dream, but another reality; a reality affirmed and consecrated in the lives lived between the pages of this month's *Heigh-Ho!* magazine.

o o o

Emma wasn't waiting any longer. The slap round the face had only served to reinforce her resolve. Perhaps she should get someone to hit her every day? She slapped herself, hard, on the other side of her face, smiling in the mirror as she did so. She started getting ready to go, to leave – if they thought a slap was going to prevent her, well, they were stupid, weren't they?

Yes, they were stupid. How did they think they could keep her here if she wanted to go away? There were at least four ways out of the house that Emma could think of. Maybe more. She just couldn't be bothered trying to think of them all. She just knew she could walk out of here any time she liked. She had a koala backpack stuffed full of money, her purse with her cheque book and a brand new credit card. There wasn't anywhere she couldn't go, at any time.

'Where do you think you're going?' her mother ran after her, wailing, as soon as she heard Emma trying to sneak out of the house.

Emma could hear the old lady's laboured breathing from beneath her blankets in the room her mother ran out of. 'Where do you think I'm going?' she said.

'I told you you weren't going anywhere,' her mother said, advancing upon her.

'Where's she going?' the old girl was trying to call, her voice thin and brittle. 'Vi! Where's she think she's going?'

'She's not going anywhere, Mum,' Violet Green called back.

'I'm going wherever I like,' Emma said, turning to fully face her mother. 'You can't stop me.'

'Oh, can't I?'

'No, you can't. You can't make me do anything against my will. What will you do, try to hit me again?'

Emma's mother reacted as if she had already forgotten that she'd struck her daughter for the first time. 'No, I – of course not. I'm sorry – Emma, please. Your Nan's not well. She's very ill. I can't – I'm sorry.'

'Yes,' Emma said, starting to go past her mother in the hall, 'so am I.'

Emma's mother looked at her. There was plenty of room for them both in the expanse of the hall there. They shared the space with a dozen or so flying cherubic ornaments, a small wilting rain forest of tropical house-plants and a couple of mock-Egyptian urns standing guard on either side of the door. Still Emma had enough room to miss her mother's touch by yards, by miles, as her mother's hand was held out towards her.

Three

She was sitting on the plane. Long haul. Business class, that's all they had available at such short notice. The seat beside her, Rob's seat, was vacant.

Four hours to go.

Emma glanced at the magazine on the vacant seat beside her. He'd flung it there before going up the aisle to the toilet cubicle. Emma sat by the window without her seat belt on trying not to concentrate on going to sleep. She tried the headphones again. No good. The songs had all been round before, several times. There wasn't another movie on for ages. Anyway, she'd seen them all. Her stomach was upset, but she felt hungry.

But, she was on her way back to New York. Rob's seat was vacant beside her.

New York, New York! Last time, when she went there with Eddie, it had been like nothing on earth. Money talks in a native New York uptown accent. Money allows stardom there. It celebrates celebrity. Eddie and Emma had stepped out in style that wonderful night they had spent uptown. The restaurant they went to, the way people looked at them, the way they spoke to them. There was no place like it.

In New York, people actually accepted you for what you were. The hotel manager had greeted Eddie as if he were filthy, stinking rich, naturally accepting the class that was money. It was the same with the headwaiter, or *maître d'*, in the restaurant.

The restaurant. You couldn't get a seat there usually, not just like that. You had to go on a waiting list for half your lifetime, or you had to marry the manager or you had to be a film star or president of the United States. But they'd got a table, they had got in. Eddie did it.

Absolutely everyone was there. You've never seen so many celebs in one place. It was like *Heigh-Ho!* brought to life. Emma just sat there with her mouth hanging open. She couldn't believe it when – you'll never guess – Tom Banks, *the* Tom Banks the movie star – who's there with his wife Angelica and another man – when *the* Tom Banks actually looks over at Emma and her dad and nods.

Emma was looking at Eddie as he nodded back. Her mouth was hanging so far open all the people waiting for tables at the entrance could see the colour of her tonsils. 'Do you know him?' she was whispering to Eddie.

She watched as Eddie raised his hand to wave at Tom. 'No,' Eddie whispered back. 'I know the fella with him. He's with *Heigh-Ho!*'

'He's coming over!' Emma hissed. Angelica, wearing the utmost loveliest of low dresses, actually walked over to their table as Tom Banks – Tom Banks! – shook hands with Eddie Green.

'Hi,' Tom was saying. 'You're Eddie Green, aren't you?'

'Yeah,' Eddie was saying, in something like an American accent, 'that's me.'

'Big winner,' Tom Banks said.

'Yeah,' drawled Eddie, 'that's me.'

'This is Angelica,' Tom Banks said, introducing his perfectly beautiful wife. As if, *as if*, he had to. Angelica smiled at Eddie and at Emma. Emma nearly died. 'And', Tom Banks said, glancing at the man from *Heigh-Ho!* before looking at Emma, 'this must be – don't tell me – Emma?' Emma really really really did nearly die. She couldn't breathe properly. Eddie was laughing. Tom Banks was holding out his hand to Emma to shake. Angelica was smiling at her.

'I really liked your film,' Emma found herself saying as she shook Tom Banks by the hand. Everyone was smiling at her.

'Thank you,' the film star said. 'Which one, in particular?'

Emma tried to think. She couldn't think of a single film that Tom Banks had been in. 'All of them,' she said. The film star and the film star's wife laughed. Eddie laughed. So did Emma.

'Well, thank you again,' Tom Banks said to her, finally letting go of her hand. 'That's very nice of you, Emma.'

○ ○ ○

She was back on the plane. Tom Banks the film star knew her and her father. *Heigh-Ho!* magazine had arranged the table at the celeb's restaurant for them and had introduced them to Tom and Angelica Banks. Now she was known in New York. All the important people must know of Eddie and Emma Green. That was what she had wanted to show Robbie. She wanted to show him the other side, life after the big leap. Emma knew it existed. She wanted to show Rob, that was all. That was all.

But Rob had made a fool of her. And she was *such* a fool. She couldn't bear to think of how he'd treated her, how she'd fallen for his niceness and his good looks. She was such a fool.

She looked at the magazine thrown on to his aeroplane seat. The latest edition of *Heigh-Ho!* lay flung open, heavy with the smiling faces of the celebs. *Heigh-Ho!* showed you through to the other side, life after the leap. That's what she could have shown Robbie: *Heigh-Ho!* including their own faces in the inner folds of its very important pages.

That's what no one else seemed to understand. Other than Eddie, nobody was capable of understanding anything. Anything at all! Emma looked away. She called the air hostess as she went by, asking for a cup of tea and a couple of digestive biscuits.

'Coffee and cookies?' the hostess said.

Emma's stomach was churning. She needed something to settle her. 'Tea and cookies, please,' Emma said.

The hostess smiled. 'Sure,' she said.

Emma looked up the aisle to the toilet cubicle. It had been engaged for an awfully long time. She didn't feel too good. She wished she could stop thinking, going over and over everything that had happened. She wished she could just sleep. All round her people were wrapped in blankets, unconscious. Not Emma. That kind of relaxation wasn't with her on this journey. It was the excitement, she supposed. Yes, it was the excitement. She settled back in her blanket. But the air-conditioning outlet above her head kept blasting cool then cold blusters of air at her face. It reminded her too much of that house in which she was supposed to live in luxury with her parents.

Emma picked up the edition of *Heigh-Ho!* from the seat next to her own. She leafed through the pages and pages of captioned photographs, shuffling quickly through to the set featuring herself and her little, happy family.

There they all were, in *Heigh-Ho!* magazine. Out of everything that had happened that day, out of all the action and excitement, the arguments, fights, the pool-plunges and illicit water-liaisons, what did they do?

They did Violet Green indoors with porcelain ornaments and grandmother's best china. They did fixtures and fittings, homes and gardens. If you looked closely, very closely, you could just make out Emma leaving the old house. If you looked even more closely at the next set, if you magnified and exaggerated the facial features, you could maybe see Emma and her friends bobbing in the new pool on a sunny day. Bobbing like pleased schoolchildren they were, or seemed, in the folds of the interior blandness of the latest edition of *Heigh-Ho!*

What was the point? It showed them like any ordinary family blinking stupidly into the camera, bemused by their own good fortune.

What was the point? Everything that had happened that

day had been ignored. They could have been anybody there, smiling and nice and bobbing happily in the swimming pool as if that was all there was to it.

What was it with these magazines? Didn't they want a good story? What about the personalities behind the good fortune? Without them, it wasn't worth anything. Who would want to read this rubbish anyway? Emma threw *Heigh-Ho!* on to the vacant seat beside her. She felt betrayed by them all. By everyone. They all wanted to make her ordinary. What was it with everyone? Why didn't anyone understand? Why didn't anyone in the whole world understand one single thing of what she was about? Only Eddie, dancing with the most beautiful and most famous of the world's women in an exclusive restaurant in New York – only he could have a single clue just how it felt to do that, and then have to live like this.

Eddie was probably dancing right now in Spain, or wherever he was. Nobody really knew for sure. He was answerable to no one. He was rich. He could go wherever he liked, whenever, without any explanation. He was free.

And his daughter was going to be like that. Exactly like that.

o o o

The aeroplane engines thrummed through her popping ears. Emma seemed to start awake without actually having fallen asleep. The chair beside her was still vacant. She looked down the aisle. Nobody stirred.

The air hostess wasn't coming back. Emma was trying to sleep without her tea and biscuits, without coffee and cookies, without a hope. The shape of the chair she was in wouldn't allow her to put her head back far enough. She couldn't sleep in this position, crunched forward like this. She couldn't clear her head of images, of recollections of conversations, arguments, insults. She turned to look back up the aisle to see where the hostess had got to. But she could see him there instead, coming back to take up his seat beside her. Emma watched his approach. She looked at his big business suit flapping open, the overhang of his business-lunch belly.

He picked up the discarded copy of *Heigh-Ho!* offering it to Emma. 'Like a read?' he said, smiling, perspiring.

Emma turned away. She swallowed her tears. Why could she not just leave the afternoons, the evenings, the long, lost nights behind her? This aeroplane must have been dashing forward in time at hundreds of miles an hour. Why could she not just leave it all, leave England and everyone still in it, far away in the distances of time? She could feel the cold dread of the air-conditioning against her face as she tried not to feel sick, alone on the aeroplane flight to New York City. Alone, but with an oversized American business baron drinking and sweating in the seat next to her where Rob should have been.

o o o

Emma was feeling terrible, terribly alone and afraid and trying not to cry. It was because she couldn't sleep, she supposed. She was getting over-emotional.

The man at the ticket desk had made her look such a fool. 'Concorde?' he had said. 'Concorde to New York?'

'Yes, please,' Emma had had to stand at the front of the ticket-desk queue saying.

'But, haven't you heard? Concorde's grounded.'

'Grounded?'

'Yes. No more flights. There was a crash. Haven't you heard anything about it at all? Where have you been?'

Emma wasn't sure now where she'd been. Everything seemed so mixed up and confused. All of the emotions attached to events were jumbled, as was the sequence of the events themselves. Somehow events had so influenced her that she seemed to be taking this flight through no will of her own. Something had been shoving her to one side of her own life. America should have felt like the home from home to which to run. But America snored heavy and intoxicated in the seat beside her, with a copy of her feature-spread edition of *Heigh-Ho!* spread out across its big belly.

The air hostess finally brought her some tea and cookies. Emma's head was swimming. She tried to eat, but couldn't clear her mind of the sickening images of running from the Italian café with Claire Thomas and Helen coming out of Mallory's to watch her. She felt the madness of her dash to the taxi-rank, the hysteria of the ride home, the bitterness of the argument with her mother.

Emma could still feel the sting of her mother's work-hardened hand across her face. She could feel the humiliation of standing at the front of the queue at the ticket desk being patronised because Concorde had failed.

Concorde had failed.

Her feature in *Heigh-Ho!* was a travesty. The first and most prestigious supersonic aeroplane in the world had crashed, and *Heigh-Ho!* was a travesty. Fate seemed determined to deal Emma some very nasty and very violent blows.

Four

It was so exciting the first time Emma had travelled in a yellow taxicab. 'Yes, sir,' the driver had exclaimed, happy to take a fare to the Grand Central Hotel. 'Yes, sir,' he had said, practically running round the big yellow car.

Now when Emma said it, the driver eyed her suspiciously, leaning against the fender of the car with an unlit cigarette between his fingers. 'Can you take me to the Grand Central Hotel?' she said, approaching him with nothing but the clothes she stood in and her invaluable backpack.

He inspected the cigarette end, seeming surprised that it remained unlit. 'Yeah? You want for me to take you to the Grand?' Emma nodded. 'Is that so?' he said, his head tilted to one side in slow curiosity. 'How you gonna pay?'

Emma already felt intimidated, just being here on her own. She had to keep telling herself that all she had to do was turn round and catch another plane back home. It was as easy as taking the bus. This is no different from being in London, she was trying to tell herself. But as soon as she left the airport, the taxi driver looked at her, taking an unlit cigarette from his mouth as if he was deciding whether or not to do her harm. She had to show him cash, American dollars, before he'd allow her into his cab.

'The Grand?' he said again, as he got into the driver's seat.

'Yes, please,' she said. There was no mistake. She was here, in New York, intending to stay at the Grand Central.

But the man at the reception desk at the Grand looked at her suspiciously as she stood there with nothing but her koala backpack. Last time, arriving with Eddie, a bellboy, actually wearing a uniform with a little pillbox hat, had scuttled to get their bags. Eddie had tipped everyone in sight. 'Yes sir, Mr Green sir,' the bellboy had said. 'Miss Green?' he'd said, taking Emma's one bag from her.

'Miss Green?' the man at the reception now eyed her and said, as if there had been some kind of a mistake. 'And do you have a reservation?'

'No, I – didn't think I'd need one. Do I? I've stayed here before.'

'I'm sorry, Miss Green,' the man said. 'We really don't have any vacancies. I'm sorry.' Emma faltered at the reception, wondering what to do next. Why was New York eyeing her so suspiciously all of a sudden? 'You're, ah, just over from London, Miss Green?' the man said.

'Yes. But I've stayed here before. With my father.'

'Oh. Well, I'm sorry, Miss Green. You should book, you know? You shouldn't really just come to town, you know, without booking.'

'I didn't – have the time.'

'Ah. I see. You didn't have the time. Are you okay? Can I get you something?'

'No. Thank you. I'm very tired. I need a room, and a bath. I need to sleep.'

'Look,' he said, 'I'll tell you what I can do. I have a little unofficial arrangement with the Excelsior. Should I get you a room there? It's a good hotel.'

'Yes, please. That'd be lovely.'

He smiled. 'Just over from London, eh?'

'Yes.'

'Yeah. London. What a town. It must be great, living in London town?'

'Well you know, I don't actually –'

'Yeah. London town.' He lowered his voice. 'Listen, I can get you a room. Listen – excuse me, sir,' he turned and said to a man at the reception counter, 'be with you in just a minute.'

His voice lowered again. 'Miss Green, the Excelsior. You'd like me to get you a good room? They got some good rooms. Listen, a good friend of mine can fix it for you – have a nice day, now,' he said as a woman handed over one of the room keys. His voice lowered again. 'A hundred, we'll have you fixed up, good. Yeah. Okay? – Have a nice day, now – be with you in a minute there, sir – leave it to me, Miss Green. Have you fixed up downtown in a minute. Yeah – thank you. Thank you, sir. You have a nice day now. And you, sir. Thank you.'

He turned to Emma. 'I'll get the doorman to call you a cab. We'll soon have you fixed up. A hundred, yes. That's it. That's just fine. Now, how is old London Town?'

o o o

Another cab ride, always another cab ride. Robbie had preferred to take the bus and train. Now Emma in another yellow cab took too long a ride through too many New York backstreets. 'Is it very much further?' she had to lean forward to ask her driver. He, however, did not seem to understand English too well. The ID screwed to the back of his seat said that his name was Rodriguez. 'Mr Rodriguez?' Emma said.

He pulled over, quickly, turning round as if Emma had accused him of something. She felt afraid. She was too tired to deal with this. She couldn't understand what was going on with these drivers, what they were expecting of her. Emma found herself pinned to the seat by Mr Rodriguez's stare. 'Is it – can you tell me how far it is to go?' she said.

He stared at her. 'Excelsior?' he said. 'Here?' he said, looking about. 'No. Excelsior. Si?'

'Si. Please,' she said.

'Okay. Excelsior. Okay.'

o o o

The Excelsior had radiators. Across the street, a building was being demolished. A whole wall fell to the single swing of a huge metal ball on a chain hung from a crane. Mr Rodriguez swung away from the kerb, from the sidewalk, in a great haste from the flying dust.

Emma checked into her room in a hurry. She was expecting to be expected, but was not. They knew nothing about her, but, yes, there were rooms available. Emma checked in as quickly as she could. She needed desperately to lie down in the dark. She needed to breathe and not to think.

The bath she had to lie in was huge and would have taken an hour or more to fill half-way. The water merely dribbled from the taps. A limescale stain striped the back of the bath. Everything was massive, cumbersome. The room had radiators, overstuffed ancient-looking furniture, twenty-foot high ceilings and windows that wouldn't open, but never quite managed to close. She splashed herself damp in about three inches of water before collapsing into the deep, deep softness of just about the biggest bed she'd ever seen.

She was trying not to remember where she was. But the gap in the curtains in both windows let in the white-hot light of New York City, the spaces in the windows crunched with the dust and the din of the demolition workers. One of them seemed to be in her room, shouting. 'Hey! Hey! Hey!'

A dumpster chugged backwards and forwards under her window-sill. Somewhere in the hotel a telephone was ringing. 'Hey! Hey! Over here! Hear me? Here! Here! Here!'

The temperature in the room was rising with the curtains closed. The great grill of a radiator started to knock, as if there was a prisoner in one of the other rooms trying to make contact with the outside world. 'Hey! Hey! Down further! Down further! Down! Down! There you go!'

Emma turned. She kicked off the single sheet she'd left covering her. 'Please be quiet,' she whispered.

New York, she was beginning to realise, didn't listen. New York talked. It shouted and hollered at the top of its voice. 'Hey! Hey! There you go! There you go!' A hundred dollars and you'll be fixed up in a minute. A yellow cab ride. Another cab ride.

Have a nice day, now.

It must be great, living in London town.

'Please be quiet,' she whispered to the city that never slept. 'Please be quiet.'

o o o

'Speak to Tom Banks. Tom and Angelica Banks. Speak to the people at *Heigh-Ho!* magazine. They booked a table for us before. Ask them. Emma Green. Ask Tom Banks.'

There was a weary silence down the line before the *maître d'* said, 'Listen. Lady, if Tom and Angelica don't have no reservation, they don't get no table. Hear me? Lady, this ain't England, you know? You know?' The line went dead.

Emma held the heavy leg-bone of a telephone receiver to her ear. She was sitting at the table in her room, the number-dial type telephone set before her. The line to the celeb's restaurant had gone dead in her ear. 'Lady, this ain't England, you know?' She dropped the heavy handset into its cradle. The telephone dinged, once. 'I know,' she said.

This ain't England, this ain't. Emma didn't have a clue what she was supposed to be doing here, or where exactly she was, other than being definitely not in England. She couldn't remember or work out exactly what day this was. She picked up the telephone handset again. The thing was so heavy, it was making her arms ache. It was making her head ache. And her back and legs.

She had slept, in the end, but with a fitfulness through the clank and body-heave of meat-market deliveries round the bend and just up the road to the dumpster track. She had slept through the shouts of the hardhats, through the demolition of a building, of a whole city. She had had to get up and turn on a vast TV set on the far wall.

The city was falling about her ears. She leapt awake to the sound of traffic accidents, a passionate argument, to muggings, murders, to a police arrest. The television set was still on. A blue light was flashing on and off outside her window. The *maître d'* at the celeb's restaurant wasn't in any mood to listen to her. The telephone rang with a single strange ding, the dialling tone a foreign, unwelcoming grind into the inner ear. Emma found herself unbearably hungry, with the weight of the huge telephone cradled in the crook of her neck and shoulder. American football was being enacted on the television screen that filled practically all the far wall. Padded men were flying into each other for the sake of it. They clumped together. Emma ached all over.

She rang down to the reception desk to ask if they could book a table for her in a decent restaurant somewhere. 'You want that I should book a table in the restaurant?' the receptionist said.

'Yes, please,' Emma said. The lines of men on the TV screen pounded into each other. Part of the city fell into dust and rubble on the ground. The rows of dumpsters chugged into the dead city. Frozen meat wagons delivered ever more dead city cargo round the bend.

'You don't need a reservation for the restaurant,' Emma vaguely heard the receptionist telling her. 'Residents don't need a reservation. You want that I should send you up a menu?'

Emma found herself vaguely flicking through the television channels. More police sirens, gunfights, indigenous people on horseback savagely body and face painted, an arrow through the heart of white America. 'Yes, please,' Emma heard herself saying. 'I want that you should send me up a menu. Yes, please.'

'French cuisine,' the receptionist was saying.

'That'll be fine,' Emma said, letting drop the heavy receiver back into the singly dinging cradle of the telephone. Everything in the room seemed to belong to an age before this one, a heavier, more stable world in which people knew how long they wanted things to last.

Walls were falling outside Emma's hotel window. Married couples were having private, intimate rows on the television on the far wall, the heavy taps were all furred up and the drapes were clogged and creaked with dead city dust.

o o o

French cuisine. Which didn't stop the old lady over there bringing in her German sausage-dog and feeding it every now and then with semi-masticated meat from her mouth.

Emma had no clothes to change into. She had tried to take a shower under the green gelatinous fluid that dripped from the showerhead. In the end, she had floated again on a few tepid inches of water in the rasping limescaled bath. She had dressed once more in the clothes in which she'd arrived.

The old lady with the sausage-dog eyed her as she was shown to a vacant table amidst a sea of vacant tables. It looked like the restaurant on the *Titanic* after the event. Emma was given another copy of the menu. She studied the translations from the French. Another old couple drifted in, sole-survivors. The sausage lady watched them with cadaverous, drowned eyes. A slippery waiter appeared from nowhere at Emma's elbow to enquire if she would like to order a drink. All Emma could think to do was to emulate Eddie and ask for some champagne.

The waiter's face showed for a moment the ghost of a smile. 'Then, perhaps,' he said in an elaborately English accent, 'some oysters, to accompany? Particularly fitting, I always think, don't you?'

'Yes,' Emma said, trying to see where the oysters were on the menu.

The waiter glanced and nodded at the old couple as they settled behind their menus on a nearby table. They had chosen to sit so close, Emma felt even more embarrassed. All these empty tables and there they all were, huddled together like survivors.

'And then to follow?' the waiter was saying to Emma. She was desperately scanning the menu. All she really wanted was a burger and chips and a diet coke. The old couple were listening, she could tell. They were waiting to hear what she was going to say to the waiter. 'Perhaps', he leaned closer to her and whispered, 'I might suggest the Number Eighteen to follow. I think you'll find it particularly palatable.'

'Yes,' Emma said, handing him the menu, 'that'll be fine. Thanks.'

The old couple were watching her as the waiter set up an ice-bucket next to her table, showing her the label on the bottle of champagne. They watched the cork being popped. Emma had to taste the stuff. She pretended to like it. The waiter poured for her. The old couple watched her drink some more.

She sat there.

The sausage lady regurgitated some more meat, sliding it under the table.

The old lady with her husband was surrounded by rows of pearls. She had painted-on lips and doll-blue painted eyes. She was whispering something to her whitehaired partner. He looked over at Emma. She felt obliged to taste some more champagne.

'Pardon me?' he said. Emma smiled. She thought that perhaps he'd burped or something, accidentally. 'Pardon me?' he said again. Emma tried looking politely away. She could feel them blinking at her. The sausage lady chewed for her dog. 'Pardon me?' the whitehaired man said again.

'That's okay,' Emma said, embarrassed, 'we all have to do it, every now and then.'

The old man looked at his painted lady-wife. 'Excuse me?' he said, looking back at Emma. 'Excuse me?'

'That's all right,' Emma said, 'really. Honestly, I don't mind.' But the old couple were staring at her as if she was an imbecile. The sausage lady was blinking over at them, chewing a hot dog.

The old man put out his hand. 'Mr and Mrs Charles Henderson,' he said.

But the waiter was wending his way quickly back through the empty tables with a silver tray supporting eight dreadful looking crusty objects he'd scraped off the bottom of a boat. 'Oysters!' he announced, setting down the silver tray. Emma, without a chance to accept Mr Henderson's hand, peered at the monstrous darkness inside the barely opened crustacean shells. 'Mr and Mrs Henderson,' the waiter was saying to the old couple, 'I'll be with you in just a moment.'

The lady with Mrs Henderson's face painted on was patting her hair. It all moved together, every part of it, in one lacquered lump. 'Well!' she exclaimed. Whitehaired Mr Henderson was clearing his throat, making a great show of straightening his napkin.

Emma looked up at the waiter.

'Enjoy,' he said, with relish.

o o o

'The world's your heavily pearled oyster, my dear,' Eddie Green had once said to his daughter.

Now the pearls hung heavy in a chain-link round the turkey neck of Mrs Charles Henderson as Emma was quietly consuming oysters as if she was lapping up the world. They were repulsive. They were like solid snot you had to swallow in one go. But the best was supposed to be the best, right? And Emma had to do it right, and do it in style.

She was having to drink the champagne, because she could. A whole bottle in an ice bucket. How disgusting was that? Champagne and oysters? She felt like throwing up. All she wanted was her burger and chips, a proper cold drink with some sweetness to it. But the revolting oysters slithered down screaming, because they were still alive, while the champagne shouted in her mouth almost with a soreness of dry iced bubbles. The whole thing was just too disgusting. The other three diners watched her doggedly. Emma had to act the little rich girl out on the town on her own. She had to drink the champagne. She had to try to look confident, comfortable with herself. They studied her, these gawping restaurant monsters. The waiter waited, smiling, patronising her. She kept her shaking hands firmly in her lap, working quickly now and then at prising open another oyster shell. The repulsive snot-creature seemed to cringe as the air attacked it. Emma had to swallow that.

The something French from the menu that the waiter had chosen for her appeared as her next course. Emma couldn't remember what it was supposed to be. She hadn't a clue. All she knew was that it was very expensive. Four hundred dollars you could do in here, by yourself, quite easily.

Emma looked about. Thirty years ago, this place must have had style. She looked at Mrs Henderson's caked make-up. Thirty years ago, *she* had style. She and this hotel had aged together, their dream of class gradually tarnishing and curling at the edges, but still dressed in an inappropriate and disgraceful expense.

The next course sat sloppily on a huge dish before her. Some unidentifiable objects drifted lost in a light brown sauce. It tasted of dead fungus and garlic. Everything tasted of dead fungus and garlic. That was all there was to it. Emma started trying to look round at what the others had on their plates.

Everything was swimming in sauce. It all tasted of fungus and garlic. Nobody was eating anything they liked, judging by the look on the Hendersons' faces. They all had a nasty flavour in their mouths, a horrible stench under their noses. The sausage lady spat it all out.

The cutlery Emma had to use was huge, silver, practically useless. It was a wonder someone didn't bust their mouth open on some great lump of eating metal. The ceilings were so high, the curtains heavy with dust. Nobody could have really wanted to eat here. This place would ruin anybody's appetite.

Emma had to try not to look at what was on her plate. What, didn't French people have any teeth or something? Surely everyone in France didn't have everything swimming in garlicked baby-sick, did they?

o o o

Emma sat trying to swallow what she could. She had to show these people. As much as she wanted a glass of cold water, she kept on with the champagne until she had a bit of a headache and had begun to feel slightly nauseous.

The only good thing about the meal was the ice-cream that turned up afterwards. It was mint chocolate and lovely. The loveliest ice-cream Emma had ever tasted. She breathed a sigh of relief at its coldness, its purity of flavour. It seemed to settle everything inside her, everything that had been swallowed like medicine, turning her stomach. But before she'd had a chance to finish the ice-cream, the smiling waiter had come over and poured out some black steaming coffee into the little cup by her plate. Emma felt obliged to drink some of it. It was nearly strong enough to bite into. The cream she added swirled on the top as if it didn't want to get involved. The yellow cream stuck to her top lip, while the dense black coffee coated the inside of her mouth. It felt like eating coffee powder straight from the jar.

145

'Is there anything else we can get for you?' the waiter sidled over and said.

'No,' she said, 'no, thank you.'

Then, as he was about to turn away, she quickly said, 'I'm going to need a cab. I'm going out, to – can you get someone to call me a cab?'

Emma watched him smile, slowly, patiently. 'The doorman can do that for you, Miss Green.'

'Oh', she said, 'thanks. I'm – er – going to a club. I need – is there someone that could possibly –'

'The receptionist can advise you on suitable venues of entertainment, Miss Green,' he said, his slow patient eyes actually closing for a few moments.

'Right. Reception. Right. Thanks.'

'Is there anything else?'

Emma shook her head. She felt intimidated. All at once she couldn't face the faces of the other diners. She felt invaded and victimised by the etiquette in common here, by the heaviness of cutlery and curtains and by the over-rich sauces and curdled cream on the coffee. She sat blinking, swallowing, trying to breathe, wondering how to get up and leave this place. She sat awkwardly, wishing Rob was here to lick the ice-cream bowls with her, to spit in the fat faces hovering like moons over her.

The waiter came back at her, threatening her with more coffee. 'No!' she said, too loudly. 'Nothing more. Thank you. I need to –' she stammered, getting up. She picked up her koala backpack and left the restaurant. She felt wobbly, tired and foolish with their eyes at her back. Please don't let me trip, she was thinking. Please don't let me stumble and fall. She was feeling very wobbly indeed. The air felt full of particles, bits of powdered fungus and garlic, droplets of coffeed cream.

'I need a cab,' she blurted out at the man on the reception. 'I need a cab to take me to a club.'

'Pardon me?' he said.

'Oh,' said Emma, trying to breathe properly. 'Can you call me a cab,' she said, swallowing her coffee and cream saliva.

'A cab?' he said, as if surprised by the request.

'Yes, a cab. I'd like to go to a – club. You know, a good one. Where celebs go.'

'Celebs?' he said.

The light was shining in Emma's eyes. She was still eating French coffee. 'Yes, celebs. You know, celebrities. I want to go to one of those clubs where celebrities go.' The receptionist stared at Emma. She couldn't breathe properly, with the lights shining and the receptionist staring into her like that. She couldn't breathe in, couldn't think. 'They told me you'd know,' she said. 'They told me in the restaurant you'd know all the right places to go.'

'They did? Did they say that?'

'Yes, they did. Don't you know?'

He shook his head. 'I'm terribly sorry, Miss Green. I don't know anything about celebrities. Who did you have in mind, exactly?'

'Nobody! No, look, nobody specific. Why's it so hot in here?'

'Is it?'

'Yes. Look, please. Can't you just get me a cab?'

'The doorman –'

'Ah! Right,' said Emma. 'Right. The doorman.'

She turned. 'The doorman,' she said again as she turned away from the door and swept across the reception to the ladies' lavatories beside the bar. She burst in, breathing hard, sweating. She dashed over to one of the open cubicles, kneeling over the clean white toilet bowl. Four hundred dollars worth of French cuisine came up looking exactly as it had when it had been served to her, only remixed and with at least twice as much garlic aroma.

The taxicab driver licked his lips. Emma could smell gasoline on his breath. She was in the back breathing the cheap imitation leather of the cab seats. Outside it had started to rain. A shiver of pale dread ran over Emma's wearied body. She still tasted like slops, like the ruin of a simple digestive system. She shivered under the oily gaze of another taxi driver.

'You want the truth?' he was saying. 'You wanna know the truth? I'll tell you the truth. The Big A ain't what it was, if you want the truth. Time was – gah – what the – I'll tell you something,' he said, looking back at Emma. 'Shall I tell you something? Disco's dead. Forget it. You wanna good night out in New York, you know what to do?' He glanced back. 'You stay in, that's what you do. You stay in.'

The driver fell silent. Emma waited. 'Slingback's, you say?' she ventured.

'Yeah,' he said. 'Yeah. Slingback's. If anyone's going anywhere in New York, it's Slingback's. You want I should take you there?'

Emma said, 'Yes please.' They stopped at the lights. 'Don't Walk' changed to 'Walk', by the side of the road.

'You gotta know your way round,' the driver said. 'Yep.'

Emma was silent. She wanted to work out how to open the window, but having to concentrate on looking for a handle was making her feel more queasy. She tried to focus past the driver on to the road ahead.

'Yeah,' the driver was saying, half turning in his seat. 'Slingback's. That's where they're all going at the moment. That's the place to go, at the moment. Film stars. Rock stars.

Yeah. I've seen them all, right in the back of this taxi, right here. Right where you're sitting, just last week, the guy from – you know, that TV? You know? Where you can win a million dollars? Yeah, him. Right where you're sitting now. Just last week. Hey, I wouldn't mind winning a million dollars, you know?'

'Or twenty-three million pounds,' Emma said.

He glanced in his mirror at her. She tried not to look at him. She was having to hold on to the approaching road, but they were turning so many corners it was dizzying. So many, many corners. 'No,' he said, 'no one don't win no twenty-three million. Only a million,' he said. 'Still, a million bucks is a million bucks, yeah?'

'Yeah,' Emma said.

The taxi driver fell silent. Emma could hear him thinking about what he'd do if he won his million bucks. 'There you go,' he said, pulling up outside the door of Slingback's.

Emma shot out of the cab, glad to be able to move, to feel the night air against the skin of her face. As soon as she got out, she noticed that, after a fifteen- or twenty-minute drive, she could see the Excelsior where she was staying just a few hundred yards up the road.

The taxi driver, noticing where she was looking, said, 'You gotta know your way round. You gotta know where you're going – That'll be fifty bucks,' he said. 'You have yourself a nice time now, yeah?'

○ ○ ○

There were still a few raindrops spattering here and there on the sidewalk. Emma looked up to allow one or two spats on to her face. Still, at last she was here, at Slingback's in the Big Apple, wearing her soiled designer clothes but with the koala on her back jam-packed with spending money. She approached the surprisingly small entrance door to the nightclub. There were two huge hardhead security bouncers posted at either side of the door. They were both watching her intently, seriously. Emma was going to have to walk between the gap between the two of them, which was narrow, to say the least. She headed for the slender space, which was closing down still further on her approach.

She walked straight up to them, looking up into their huge blank faces. 'Excuse me,' she said.

One of them shook his head. 'Not tonight, babe.'

Emma stood there. 'Excuse me,' she said again. 'I wish to go inside.'

His head was shaking again. 'No. I don't think so. Guests only tonight. Come back some other time. In a few years, maybe.'

Emma stalled. 'Excuse me,' she said, 'excuse me. I'm – staying at the Excelsior. Up there. I've come here especially, from England. From London.'

Their blank, uninterested faces blinked down at her.

Nothing happened. Looking up at them was starting to make Emma feel dizzy again. From somewhere inside the building, an extractor fan was belching out cigarette smoke. But the huge hard faces remained unaffected by her. She took off her backpack.

'You don't understand,' she said. 'What you don't – you don't know what I've got in here,' she said, holding out the bag.

They faltered, glancing at each other. Then the first one shook his head. 'Guests only tonight,' he said.

'What's wrong,' Emma stammered. She looked from one to the other. 'Can't you speak or something?' she said to the silent one. He looked down at her, powerfully uncommitted.

Opening her bag, about to put her hand in, Emma said, 'There's a lot of money in here.' The cigarette smoke from the extractor blew straight into Emma's face. She had to close her eyes for a few moments. She wanted to open them to find the whole of New York razed by demolition dumpsters from the face of the earth.

'Is your name on the list?' the first one was saying to her.

She opened her eyes. The bouncers still stood over her like skyscrapers. 'I've got an awful lot of money in here,' she said.

'Is your name on the list?' the first one said again.

The second one glanced at him. 'She's packin,' he said.

'Yes,' she said, 'I'm packing. And my name's on the list. My name's Emma Green. My father's on every guest list in New York. So am I.'

The one that did most of the talking was shaking his closely shaven head again. 'I don't think so, baby. Not tonight.'

'You don't want to stop me,' she said, holding the bag up to the other one, 'do you?'

The two bouncers glanced at each other. The first one said, 'Not tonight.'

'You can't stop me, just like that. My father's name's Eddie Green. He's a good friend of Tom Banks, the actor. If my dad gets on the telephone to –'

'Hey, hey,' the talkative one was saying as a car was pulling up behind Emma, 'listen to me. Listen to what I'm saying to you, baby. You are not –' Emma noticed the second bouncer tapping his partner on the arm. She looked round to see the door of the limousine opening. A man was stepping out.

As she looked at him, he strode up to the darkly suited security bouncers. 'Big Al!' he shouted at the first bouncer, holding up a high-five.

Big Al slapped the hand, grinning. 'Hey, we've been wondering when you were coming back,' Big Al said. 'What's been keeping you away so long?'

'Oh, you know,' the man said, 'producing. LA, London, you know?' The bouncers were nodding as if they did. Emma noticed a tall, tall woman sliding out of the car behind them, her legs like strong, shimmering snakes. She slithered forward, taking the man's arm as Big Al the bouncer and his pal stepped back and watched them go through into the club.

Emma's head was thumping. She screwed up the koala backpack. It looked too silly here, too childish. 'You don't know who I am,' she said, do you – Al!'

Big Al stiffened. 'No,' he said, peering down at her, 'I don't.'

Emma glanced at his pal. 'Emma Green,' she said. Her head was spinning.

'Yeah,' Big Al said, 'I heard you.'

Emma stood there. She felt ill and foolish. 'Look,' she said, 'you know I've got money. You want some money,' she said to Big Al's pal, 'don't you?'

He glanced at Al. 'If she's packin',' he said. Al shook his head.

'Why not?' said his pal.

'Yes,' Emma said, 'why not?'

'She's packin', man,' Al's pal insisted, holding out a big open hand towards Emma.

'Oh, yeah?' Al said. Emma leapt. Al had snatched the bag from her hands.

'Give me that!' she screamed.

'Take it all,' Al was saying to his pal. 'You want it? Take it all. She ain't comin' in.' The two bouncers were glaring at each other.

'Give me my bag,' Emma said. The two huge doormen were still facing each other out as Al casually flung the bag high over Emma's head. Emma watched it spin and plop into the road. A passing car ran it over. 'You can't do that,' Emma said. 'You just can't treat me like that!'

'Get yourself home, little girl,' Big Al said, his face approaching Emma's.

'You just can't –' Emma was saying, just before she found herself practically picked up and flung spinning and tumbling to where her dampened and dirtied backpack lay in the road. Emma slipped and stumbled as the plump rain steamed on the surface of the road. Big Al and his pal were watching her, standing side by side.

Emma was picking up her bag, slipping across the wet surface of the road. 'I'm phoning my father,' she was saying. She looked up, almost crying. 'I'm going to get something done about you!'

'Go home now, little girl,' Al was saying, beginning to advance towards her.

Emma picked up the dead Koala. 'I hate you all,' she started to mumble, walking away from the threat that was Big Al. 'I hate you all. You're all nothing, that's what you are. You are all nothing.'

That's exactly what it all amounted to – a big nothing. Wherever she went, whatever she did, it was all a bitter, sickening disappointment. If there was still a place for excitement, a glittering future, where could it be, and who could it include? Everywhere Emma went the places were heavily curtained with their own customs and expectations erected to exclude her from the élite. Or else they were not élite, but fat and crumbly, older and more decrepit than they should have been, resistant and hostile or just plain stupid.

She stumbled up the road as the rain plumped down. What were these streets if not the smell of garbage cans and wet concrete? This was no beginning of a glittering future. The trash stank as she passed. A balding man appeared suddenly from a darkened doorway, staggering forward to retch into the gutter. Emma looked quickly away. She herself knew what it was like tonight to be sick, to be physically sick of the downtown dead-city streets. She hated New York, America, London, England. She felt repulsed by the cities and the suburbs, the streets and the housing estates. Wherever she went she was bound to be brought to nothing.

She was sick of it. Walk. Don't Walk. Don't Walk. Don't Walk.

She had suffered enough, too much. She was sick of it. She was sick. Sicker than the man vomiting in the street back there, more tired and haggard than the two streetbums wrapped in cardboard down by the waste bins over there. Emma walked on by as if she was truly battered by the streets and the club doorways and the bins and the lights going out. She marched by the two pairs of boots and shoes sticking out of the cardboard bedstead going tick tick tick with the regularity of the rain.

'Spare a dollar?' came a dislocated voice from beside the bins.

Emma stopped. She blinked. 'Yes,' she said. 'Yes, I can spare a dollar,' she said, delving into the rustling nest inside her backpack. 'I've got plenty of spare dollars. Just how many would you like me to give you?' There was much scraping and grovelling as the hidden bodies divested themselves of the cardboard in which they slept. First out, a tall grey head of rat's-tailed hair and beard. He reminded Emma of the old man she and Robbie had dressed in pinstripes back in London. 'How much, exactly,' she said, bringing out far too much money, 'would you like me to give you?'

But the tramp reached quickly forward and grabbed Emma by the wrist. The money fell into the road. Emma tried to step back. They came at her, appearing from the dark recesses, from the gutters, from the drains. Now they were night-wild and stinking of sweet wine, rushing forward towards Emma with a greedy, drunken purpose.

'She's got money!' one shouted. It was like a battle cry. Faces floated out of the darkness all round Emma. She stood back, but clawed hands clutched at her, catching in her clothing, her hair.

'No!' she cried, more afraid than ever. 'No! Let me go! Here!' she cried, trying to hand the money over. But the claws clutched at her, scratching at her skin. She envisaged the slime from behind the bins being introduced into her bloodstream. She imagined huge insects caught and weaved into the tangles of her long hair.

She screamed.

The hands pulled at her.

She screamed again.

The koala backpack disappeared. Her jacket was pulled from her. She screamed as the jacket left her. She pulled away, running away, leaving them with everything, which was nothing now that she was so afraid. She was suddenly so terrified. The streets were webbed with darkness and the threat of horror. Emma ran. The glittering dream was really a dark, dark nightmare. It made her ill, upset, agitated, confused. It terrorised her. Everything she did terrorised her in one way or another, culminating and catching up with her here, there, where Big Al and Roy still stood in the doorway watching her run by, and there, in the hostile reception of the Excelsior hotel.

Emma didn't want to be here any longer. She wanted to go home. All she wanted now was to go home. She grabbed her key from the reception, ran blindly to her room. She couldn't wait for the lift, running nearly hysterical to the fourth floor. In her room she dashed open the drawer in which she'd left her new credit card. Yes, thank God. Then she called home, wanting more than anything to hear her father's voice. But it was her mother that answered.

'Mum,' she said.

There was a pause. 'Emma,' her mother said, 'is that you?'

'Mum, of course it's me,' she cried. 'Is Dad home yet? Is he there?'

'No,' her mother said. Just that, nothing more.

Emma sniffed. She wiped her eyes. 'Mum,' she said, 'I need some help.' But there was silence on the other end of the line. 'Mum?'

'Emma, where are you?'

Emma sniffed. She couldn't bring herself to tell her mother where she was. 'I've been really stupid, Mum.'

'I know,' her mother said. Another silence came all the way to New York from England.

'Mum? Do you know where Dad is? Is he still in Spain?'

'I don't know,' her mother said. 'I don't know where my husband is, I don't know where my daughter is.'

Emma didn't say anything. She could hear a sound at the

other end of the telephone line. 'Mum? Where's my Dad?'
Her mother was crying. 'Mum? What's the matter?'

'Emma, do you care, either way?' her mother said. 'What does it matter, as long as you've got your own way? Your grandmother's in hospital now, probably for good. That's what you wanted, wasn't it?'

Emma gagged, fighting for breath. 'Mum – I –'

'And your father's gone. And if you don't know where he is or who he's with, I'm sure I'm not going to tell you. What can I tell you?'

'Mum, don't. I didn't mean –'

'Well you've got all your own way as usual, Emma. You want your father to come and help you? Well he's never going to come and help again. He's never coming back – never!'

Emma could hear her mother's sobs. Tears were falling from Emma's eyes. 'Mum. Please.' Emma could only listen to the sobs just before the line went dead. She closed her eyes, pressing the dead telephone receiver to her ear. There was no sound. Nobody was there. She dialled again. 'Mum,' she was saying, 'Mum, Dad, please answer.' The telephone at the other end of the line was ringing. Emma listened to it ring. She was alone. The ringing all that way down the line tired her out, exhausted her. It rang and rang.

Nobody answered. Emma's tears fell.

Nobody answered. They were all gone; all shifted, distorted, changed, gone from her side. Emma had never been so alone.

Five

Emma found herself alone in front of that massive house. It towered over her as she trekked round to the rear. The summer sun was still hot in the sky, glinting reflected in the slow ripples of the swimming-pool. A manicured lawn swept away to an ornamental pond and beyond that, trees. The family owned everything. Emma wondered if anyone could really own a tree? How? What did you do? Trees just were. But the Greens had wanted to own the lot. The birds on their nests were indebted to Emma's parents. The fish in the ornamental pond owed Eddie their very existence.

Emma looked up at the huge house. It had classical pillars at either side of the front and back doors. It had pillars and porticos over the garage doors. They had come to live in a miniature town hall like pretend people. They were living pretend lives in pretend, overblown premises.

Out the front, newly delivered, a new Rolls-Royce car, pure diamond white with black interior. It was a pretend car for people who had to pretend to have somewhere to go.

There was nowhere left *to* go. Possession had spoiled ambition, from the very start. It hadn't seemed that way to begin with, of course. To begin with, the tidal force of over twenty-three million pounds had swept them all away. They were all swept up in it. What had once been a small, neat family unit with two ordinary parents, one daughter and one live-in grandmother, had become the epicentre, the very eye of the storm. Emma turned away from the reflected glare of the pool back into the dense shade of the house. She couldn't bear to remember those first few weeks, the vainglorious appetites of these little, ordinary folk let loose too suddenly and with far, far too much.

Now she couldn't have stood to revisit their old house in their old street where everybody but herself still lived happily. She couldn't bear to look back into the reality of it for her friends and her family. None were there. Her family had disappeared, friends lost in the abyss between their reality and Emma's pretentiousness. Now she looked back into the summer shadow of the house and felt afraid. A white Rolls-Royce stood waiting on the gravel drive.

This is what it all comes down to, Emma had to think, picking her way through the ornamental statuettes adorning the upper garden and mass-flat of the patio. The garden furniture stood gaudy, as conspicuous as champagne in crates and white Rollers with black, black interiors.

The designer wear from New York and Paris hung just as spectacularly incongruous on Emma in the English summer sun. The unused swimming-pool shimmered too blue, the hungry fish in the pond further down the garden too fat and obscenely full in the lips.

Nothing belonged. Especially Emma. The simplicity of Emma's past seemed now further away than a foreign country, less attainable than Mars. She went from the huge garden into the huge house. Lights came on in the kitchen automatically as she passed. It was like some spaceship, with computer controls and speed-of-light warp indicators for when your toast was done.

Emma had been ordering take-aways ever since they had moved here, or else going down to the pizza parlour for a salad. She wouldn't have been able to boil an egg in among the high-tech scramble of this place. Walking through the kitchen, and it was a long walk, you always expected to hear a robot voice speak your name, or have an automaton-arm tap you on the shoulder.

It was hot outside. Inside, everything was cold. The air got thoroughly conditioned before it got this far. Air had to be in pretty good shape, with huge pecs and a six-pack, to even set foot in here. Half the air-con vents were left torn down. The spluttering air spat out bits from time to time. The electric wires had been left still hanging from the ceilings or snaking out across the floor. Whatever they'd been looking for, the technicians had been unable to find it. The poison heart of the house remained intact, spitting out clots every so often like bad lumps of electrified air.

The living-room was overpopulated with more statuettes. The place looked like a leprechaun gymnasium stalled in time. Emma suspected the frozen figurines jostled and danced demonically behind her back. She always looked quickly round to ensure that the eyes in the pictures on the walls were still and inanimate. Behind her back, she felt a devil-power frolicking, leering at her from the squirming excess of hidden energies.

The whole place felt like that. She had to try to sleep here, with a hundred neon beads blinking on and off, security detectors humming and pulsating, air-conditioners rumbling somewhere far below. The house had hidden, unseen depths in which motors and generators thrummed, squirting electrical energy into all the coils of this magnetic mansion.

The place always crackled with static electricity, wherever Emma went. She was continually being shocked into a stunned silence. Even now, as she passed across the expanse of red axminster to the front picture windows, she clicked and sparked, her split-ends sailing away from her head on charged strands of single hair.

She looked out of the window. The diamond Roller reflected all the sun's rays on the drive. It stood cool, arrogantly refined. Emma looked down the long curving drive to the entrance gates. It was such a long way, with the sun so high and bright, there was no seeing what might be there under the shadows of the trees. They owned so many trees. So many, the trees owned them. Yes, as the house kept Emma, the trees had the lie of the land. She wanted to go out. She wanted to get away from here for a while. But that walk, that long, long walk down the drive to the street somehow intimidated her. 'No,' she found herself saying, turning away from the window, 'it isn't as bad as all that. It isn't as bad as that.' It couldn't be. How should she be so completely terrorised? What had she done?

No, it was just – it was just that –

Emma shivered. Perhaps she had a cold coming. Perhaps all she was experiencing was the extremes of hot and cold between garden and house. Yes, she had a cold or the flu coming. Her limbs ached. Her skin was sore. She had a particularly nasty cold coming on.

She was not being terrorised at all. Of course not. She just did not want, could not face opening the letter she'd seen perched against the ornamental candelabra on the table. A new Rolls-Royce waited on the drive for her father. A letter waited for Emma in here, with her mother's handwriting on it. She didn't feel very well at all.

Emma,

I couldn't stay in the house any longer. There's something wrong with having too much. Houses like this do harm. They hurt.

I can't go out. I can't stay here. I'll try to call you soon. As soon as I can.

You weren't here for your Nan, neither was your father. She was asking for you. I had to do it all. I can't do any more.

Let me call you as soon as

Mum.

Emma picked up the telephone and punched in a number. She waited for the line to connect. Her mother's mobile rang from the other side of the room. She could see it lying there plugged into the charger, switched on and ready over on the side. The light on it went off as Emma replaced the telephone receiver.

She had been alone in New York, praying that the hotel would accept her credit card for cash. She'd been alone in the yellow cab to the airport, desperately alone in first class on the plane. A black cab from Heathrow home, desperate, alone.

From continent to continent, a change only in the colour of the cabs. The loneliness remained untouched in cabs and planes and cabs and isolated mansions on the edge of desperate towns and lonely suburbs. She wanted to find her mother and her father and her grandmother, to speak to them and be with them and have them with her.

But the light on her mother's mobile phone had blinked on just across the other side of the room, then had gone out. The air-con coughed and spluttered over Emma's shoulder, like an unwelcome intruder.

o o o

She found herself looking out of the window again. Time after time she found herself squinting through the sunlight reflected from the roof of the Rolls-Royce, peering at the dark space beneath the horse chestnut trees at the other end. Was there anything else there, beyond the trees? Or was this it? You could drive yourself mad like this. You could go insane at midday in the living-room of a big house under the sun in the middle of the week. Or was this the weekend again?

She picked up the telephone again, calling Directory Enquiries to ask the girl on the other end what day it was. All days were the same to Emma now. She had so often been surprised to find it was a Sunday, with most of the shops shutting. It seemed so absurd to have the days behaving differently, as if there was something inherent in them to make these changes. All days were the same. It was only people that changed. The girl on the other end sounded surprised, but confirmed that yes, it was the weekend, and the time was half-past eleven on a hot day in late August. 'Now,' she asked Emma, 'is there a number I can get for you?'

'A number?' Emma found herself saying, having quite forgotten who she was talking to.

'A telephone number,' the girl's voice said. Emma didn't answer. She had forgotten to whom she had been speaking, forgetting that people did things, had to do things every day to make a living. It was too easy to forget the ordinary world when you lived in such a rarefied atmosphere as this. 'Hello?' the enquiries girl said. 'Caller? Are you still there?' Emma could hear her speaking, but she was not there. Her attention had been drawn from trying to remember why she had telephoned in the first place, to the trees way down the other end of the drive. 'Hello? Hello?' the telephone voice in her hand was speaking into her ear. 'Caller? Are you still there?'

'Yes,' she said, softly, almost silently. 'I'm still here.'

'Is there a number I can get for you?' Emma was peering down the drive to the faraway entrance. She shivered in the February-house at the far end of August. 'Are you still there, caller?'

'Yes,' Emma said, softly.

'Is there a number I can get for you?'

'A number?'

'A telephone number.'

'Oh. No. Thank you.'

'Then I have to cut you off – caller? I have to cut you off – goodbye.' The blankness of phone-line silence pressed against Emma's ear, speaking of nobody left to turn to. She replaced the dead, useless telephone receiver. The dead, ionised silence rushed cold at her.

The white Rolls-Royce stood in the constant sunshine like an invitation to a wedding.

Emma stepped away from the window. She let her mother's

letter fall on to the dining-table, went into the hall. The delivery documents and the keys to the new car were there on the table over which a plastercast gossamer fairy-nymphette floated like a fugitive from never-never land.

Emma felt like smashing something. She felt like crashing it all down, destroying the wasted thousands tastelessly invested here. The sweet ornaments stood bitterly begging for it. The massive computer and television sets wanted, wanted, wanted breaking. The whole house did, its armoured double glazing and security systems doing nothing to protect. Still the white of a brand-new Rolls wedded itself to the desperate opulence of the house.

Emma reached up to the plastercast fairy on a plinth above the table. Slowly, deliberately, she pushed it to the edge. She allowed it to rest, but precariously close to the drop. She looked at the car keys on the table. She looked back up at the hopeless ornament, back to the keys. She nodded to herself, picked up the keys.

Before she went out, she touched the base of the fairy. It teetered on the edge, turned slightly, fell in a last fairy flight of sheer gossamer.

Emma left it broken on the floor as she slammed the front doors behind her.

The white Rolls-Royce opened with a rich heavy-metal thunk. The corner lights blinked on and off a few times. Emma opened the door fully, climbed into the driver's seat. The door closed with the same satisfying settle of lubricated metal.

She pressed the key-button to lock the doors. Now she was safely inside. The car smelled not of new car, but of expensive black leather, of faintly perfumed deep-pile carpet.

Emma scanned the controls. Easy. A car like this would practically drive itself. Nothing to it. She put the key into the ignition, turned it to start the engine. It started as if there was no engine at all. Emma had to listen hard for the sound of it. For a few moments, all she could hear was the sound of conditioned air being brought to her across an in-car refrigerator. Emma turned off the air-con, sniffing, feeling her throat. It still felt as if she had the flu coming. She adjusted her seat. Her heart was beating hard. The cold sweat of a fever coming swept over her. She pushed the lever of the automatic drive into forward, touched one of the pedals. The car crunched forward on the drive. She touched the brake. It stopped. That was it. That was all there was to it.

Emma stepped on the pedal. The Rolls was the easiest thing in the world to drive. A Rolls-Royce was, surely, a change for the better, wasn't it?

Wasn't it?

It accelerated smoothly, quickly, quickly. Small stones from the drive were sent flying. Emma stepped on it, hurtling towards the open entrance. She screeched to a halt where the entrance met the road. She looked into the rear-view back at the house. She pulled out on to the road, turning left in front of another car that was braking hard, its horn going, lights flashing. Emma pulled away. The acceleration left the other car standing, the gesticulating driver quickly fading into the background.

Emma looked at herself in the rear-view. She was surprised to find herself crying. So she stopped. She wiped her face. She had to drive this car. This was not going to be so easy, driving through traffic, on roads with other road-users, pedestrians crossing, cyclists, the police.

She wiped her face. Up the road a way, she pulled over to find out how to operate the indicators, window-wipers, lights and horn. As she was fiddling with everything, a boy came by, stopped, looked in at her. Emma wondered if the boy recognised her, if he had any idea how old she was. She pulled away again, giving good signals, keeping her acceleration and speed down. The clothes she was wearing wouldn't give her away; they were dirty, but so obviously expensive, she belonged in a Rolls.

Well, *she* didn't. The clothes did. But now she felt ridiculous in them, in this car. She just had to get away, that was all. But she was on her own. The clothes, the car, money, bank account, none of it prevented her from crying again. The tears just fell.

She remembered her Nan, her dear old Nan saying to her that day, as she'd looked round the living-room in their old house, 'And I thought this was it.'

The tears just fell. Things had changed. They were not all right. Far from it. How could they go this far awry, this quickly? How could it happen?

o o o

The loneliness of the crowded Sunday lunchtime road frightened her. As she sat waiting in a queue of traffic, she looked into her rear-view only to find herself totally alone and conspired against. The thoroughly ordinary and every-day conspired against her, overwhelming her with hostility. She felt it all round her. The Rolls was no defence, the travesty of privilege that it now represented.

Emma was stuck in the no man's land of her own intimidated loneliness. She was confused by the one-way systems diverting her to nowhere. Which always seemed the only place she had to go. She wanted to find her family. There was a street sign instructing her to turn left. No help.

She turned. She turned again. Every car around her contained one person or more. They sat like tyrants with their driver's licences and ministry of transport certificates. Emma had nothing. She had money, which was nothing. Oh, but money has class all right. It has style. Money is as good-looking and as empty as a handsome face on a cinema screen.

Emma wanted to find her father, and her mother. She wanted to see her grandmother. Tears fell with the memory of the lovely old lady taking her by the wrist that night they found out they'd won a terrible amount of money through no fault or talent of their own. Emma hadn't known that night how she would attempt to go about being wealthy. She hadn't felt wealthy, then; she hadn't known what it was supposed by everyone to be.

What wealth was supposed to be bore no relationship to this no man's land. Emma was instructed to turn left here and right there, but that again gave no real indication of what might lie ahead. Nothing, as far as she could tell. Her grandmother was in hospital, her mother had told her so, over the telephone in New York. Emma headed towards a roundabout. A line of cars stood waiting. They all knew which lane to take, which way to turn, how to get away, how to find hospitals, parking spaces, safe havens. Emma knew nothing of the kind. She was a novice. A car like this drove itself. Emma knew nothing.

Someone on the roundabout was peering at her from the

controls of his car. Emma had veered across his lane suddenly without noticing him there. She allowed the Rolls to take control. The other driver, however, pulled alongside to glare at her before sweeping away into his exit lane.

See how they terrorised her, these people? Pulling alongside, glaring straight at her. It wasn't her fault she didn't really know what she was doing. She'd never really known what she was doing. Her grandmother had known that, had tried to tell her so. But nothing can make you listen. You look out from your own personal circumstances, using your own too-limited experience, and you make dreadful mistakes. Old people's ill-fitting dentures give such a false impression of absurdity. No wonder it was so difficult to just accept what they had to say.

It wasn't Emma's fault then, was it? Who could blame her? Her grandmother had never been rich in her life, so why should Emma have listened to her? She made dreadful, dangerous mistakes. She was driving a ton-and-a-half of expensive car along a carriageway afraid for her grandmother's life and her own sanity. You could go mad at sixteen years old with a lifetime's money in your bank account and the keys to your father's new car.

He was gone. Her mother had said she didn't know where he was. Emma suspected that Amanda from *Heigh-Ho!* would have gone with him. With him and his money. It wasn't Emma's fault then, was it? Her father was old enough to know, so how could Emma have so influenced him? Her mother had cried into the telephone to Emma, telling her that she'd got her own way, that her father was gone, her grandmother in hospital somewhere, maybe for good. Her mother sounded so upset, so *damaged*. It wasn't Emma's fault, was it? You couldn't blame her for everything, could you? Not for everything.

But as she looked at the face in the rear-view mirror, the blame for everything rested there, looking back out at her, tear-stained and full of fault. Then, as she looked away, the traffic in front had drawn to a sudden halt. The cars had all stopped in a line in front of her on the approach to another roundabout.

Her foot slammed down looking for the brake pedal. It touched the accelerator. The line of cars hurtled towards her. Her panicked foot searched again. The diamond Rolls in pure emergency performance mode, halted immediately. It just stopped, dead, rollicking on its suspension.

Emma missed the car in front. The car behind however, had no such stallion brake horsepower. A little blue family saloon populated with a little blue family screeched in a desperate smokescreen, halting only with heavy jostling contact with the back of the Rolls.

Emma's head was flung back. She was confused for a moment, unable to tell what had happened. She had stopped, then an almighty bang. She turned, looking behind. The tyre-smoke was clearing, leaving clear a view of the blue family behind in shock and a whole line of other cars behind them with drivers and passengers craning to see what had happened.

Emma turned. The people in the car in front were turning back to stare at her. She glanced in the rear-view. Men with driver's licences and insurance certificates were getting white faced from their cars. There was damage to be accounted for. Police informers were everywhere, desperate to grass.

Emma was alone in the rarefied atmosphere of the white Rolls-Royce. All around her, the hostile world of fault and blame was closing in. Everything that had happened wanted answering for here, climbing white faced from family saloons with silent, unforgiving children strapped into the back seat. Look at them, coming for her, their sanctimonious lips pressed in self-righteous indignation. Look, they were everywhere, everywhere surrounding Emma with hostility.

She couldn't stand them for a single moment longer.

The control lever of the Rolls just drifted into drive, the car itself whispering forward, swinging out of the line of shocked-face cars, gripping the ramp of the road up to the dual carriageway bypass.

The disapproval of the world receded in the rear-view and was quickly gone as the Rolls responded to the urgency driving Emma's foot into the floor. The engine did have a sound after all. It cleared its throat for performance motoring like this. Like this, it went roaring away from the towns and the other cars and all the little people. Away with them. If only forever.

If only forever. The ramp of the road gave way to the level-headed bypass. Emma swept across to the fast lane following the line of her own escape. The others would just have to keep out of her way.

She wasn't stopping now. If she did, she'd only be somewhere. This movement, the motion of increasing speed, would give no place precedent. Everywhere was merely somewhere on the way to somewhere else. And the faster you travelled, the more effectively you denied the very idea of place. So all the others would just have to watch out. There was nothing stopping her now. The fault and the blame were left behind faster, faster still.

A flashing wailing police car flew by in the opposite direction. It barely shared more than a single moment of panic in Emma's safe haven of increasing speed. This was a Rolls-Royce, a beautiful car, if slightly damaged at the back. It was a superior vehicle, providing superior performance.

Look at it go.

The bypass closed down to a single lane in each direction. Emma overtook two cars that were trapped behind the labours of a truck dirtying up the road. Emma was no longer trapped. She flew by in the full assurity of the absolute engineered power of her father's brand-new motor. She was no longer trapped by the flash of the truck's disapproving headlamps. Away with all that. Speed cleared the way. The way up ahead was a line in time, a simple exit, fatalistic and unyielding.

Away with it all. All of it.

Emma laughed. She cried. She drove the sole of her Italian shoe hard to the floor. The cars she passed gave way. They were gone to nothing.

She laughed. She was crying. The fatalistic road veered to the left. Emma dragged the car's steering into the drag of the road. Another truck coughed and belched dirty on the bend.

Emma was crying.

She followed the line. The line was laid bare for her. She had no choice. Fate dragged her weeping into the outer lane. She followed the line of her fate. Away with all that.

Away with it all. That was the past back there. Up ahead, the future, a glaring brilliance on the horizon, just a bit further ahead. Just a bit faster. Just a bit faster.

Yes. The past was dead and gone.

Fate dragged her glad and weeping once again into the outside lane.

Six

There didn't seem to be anything wrong at first.

There was white in her eyes, as blank as her memory. The white ached like time. Time to check a few things out. Like, finding the questions. Like, who was she? Her coming-to –

But this coming-to couldn't have been her own. She was too far from herself to be able to claim ownership of anything. Everything looked white. It looked like nothing, but hummed, pulsated white. It was like being born again. For a second, nothing moved. Everything was white. Perfect. For a second.

Then, the least breath of movement and a shaft of pain. Oh, yes, remember that? The newborn knows it slapping against the soles of its feet. The peace doesn't last. The newborn cries: I know! I know!

But it can know nothing but the blank white of intense pain. There is nothing else to know.

Try it. Try not knowing anything but by pain's interpretation. Try not finding a decent position in which not to find a true consciousness, try not going to the loo, try eating nothing but through your own veins. Try being afraid of the time to come when you will need to think about having to clean your teeth. Try trying not to be afraid of the time that will come when you will have to remember. Try it.

After a lifetime or so of some kind of approximate consciousness, Emma came to enough to realise the absurdity of giving everything a name. Outside of herself, outside this amorphous hurt she'd yet to reconnect to her own name, there existed objects separate in themselves. These objects somehow managed not to be a part of the discomfort. They shifted, flowed, oblivious to pain.

Occasionally an object would come to peer into her, make a moment of near contact, then float clean away without having broken through.

The air, everything, was separated into two definite halves: pain and no-pain. Sometimes she floated in pain and looked out on the alternative, sometimes vice versa, but never could the two halves now cease their co-existent balance. The names of absurd objects clicked back into memory with a little, appalling shudder through the brain. Those things out there caused a popping in here, a crackle of nerve ends electrically reconnected with a hot spark. Never had there seemed so much outside of her to cope with, to have to re-internalise. She felt a kind of horror at it all. There was so much out there, so very much to do to reconstruct herself. No one thing could possibly exist without all the others. If anything was destroyed, any one thing brought to finality, Emma was going to have to die.

She had to hold on, to it all. It was a huge, horrific task, but not nearly so horrible as losing something, which would have meant everything.

Seven

Eventually, enough fragments are pieced together on to which it is possible to iron out your abused and crumpled identity. Emma collected the fragments together in her mind, reconstructing herself piece by piece. She seemed to emerge from a teacup, the recognition of a chair, the scent of flowers on the air. As the confusion of awakening gradually, gradually subsided, then the touch of the cool clean sheets, the contact of another person's physical presence.

For a while there, for maybe a long while, Emma hadn't known a thing. The mind had become a blank white sheet, undulating with broken, crackling nerve ends. There was no memory, zero recollection of anything at all.

All she recognised for a while was pain. It was like being a child, or a tiny fledgling, hurt and afraid. But sparks of recognition gathered day by day, augmenting to a swell of certainty that began to identify the inner thing, the essence of existence that was, once again, Emma Green.

She blinked back on.

One fine day when the sudden winter weather had turned foul, Emma looked to the side and said one word.

She turned to the side and spoke, for the first time in weeks. 'Mum,' she said. Her mother cried. So did her father. He laid his face against the side of the bed and wept for her forgiveness.

Emma looked out of the window. 'What's happened to the summer?' she said, as the brown autumn wind beat a broken sway into the bare branches of the willow tree outside.

'Can you hear me?' her mother wept and said. 'Emma, can you hear me?' She tried to nod, looking up, revelling in the fact that she could see and feel and recognise her mother's face.

'Thank God!' her father said. 'Oh, thank God!' Then her father's face she could see, exactly as she remembered it. But maybe slightly older, more unrested and ravaged. But here it was, here he was, just as before.

'I've been –' Emma tried to say. But she was prevented by the onslaught rush of doctors and nurses bursting into the room to examine her and to test her faculties. Emma's mother and father held her hands, one either side, as the tests were done to ensure that she and not anyone else, had finally returned.

Emma couldn't quite work it out, before she fell asleep. She drifted easily, luxuriously, as if she hadn't slept for many, many days. Not properly, anyway. Sleep like this felt, on its verge, very rare. Emma could feel, could see the shape of it, its very roundedness falling to a soft centred perfection.

When she awoke, it was night. At least, darkness lingered at the edges of an ill-defined local light. Between the darkness and the light, her father sat slumped in a chair, asleep, a book fallen open on his lap. The wind outside wrote rain slashes across the glass of the window.

Emma went to move. She found she could not. Her limbs were tied, restricted from any movement at all by splints and straps. Even her head was confined in its movements by a high collar that cupped her jaw and chin.

There was a feeling about the room. A new sensation lingered somewhere, waiting to reassert itself. Emma tried to locate it. Where was it now? Oh yes, it was inside her. Or very nearly.

'Dad,' she said, softly. Her head could just move enough to one side to allow her to see his sleeping face in the armchair just outside the light. His slow breath sounded deep but laboured, his throat restricted by being in that awkward position sleeping in the chair. 'Dad,' she said again.

He silenced. His head came up. He blinked over at her. Emma could see his tired eyes focusing upon her face. She heard the open book on his lap flap to the floor as he leapt up. 'You're awake! Emma!' he cried. 'Don't move. I have to get the –'

'Dad,' she interrupted him, 'don't go anywhere. Stay where you are, please.' He steadied himself, standing over her. He, she could see, could hardly breathe. He was looking at, gazing into, examining her face. Emma looked up and felt from him an overwhelming strength of feeling towards her. She watched him beat a path through his emotions to eventually force a smile for her. His mouth quivered. Two tears dropped soundlessly from his eyes on to Emma's bedcovers.

'How are you, my daughter?' he said, slightly shaking his head. 'How are you Emma, my daughter?' Emma watched his hand move to touch her so gently, so very gently on the cheek. They left it a long, long time, a very long time before any other words were spoken. It felt right for nothing to be said between them. They looked at each other.

Then Emma's father smiled. His tears freely fell. 'You don't know,' he whispered, 'nobody knows just how good it is to hear your voice.'

o o o

Emma fell asleep again. Sleep came and took her away whenever it felt like it. But now she dreamed.

She dreamed of falling over the edge of a precipice. The sudden jolt of the fall awakened her in pain.

Every time she woke, the world changed a little. The light turned round, certain smells associated themselves with morning, afternoon and evening. But mostly, the internalised world, herself, was altered. The pain of having to reassemble everything external to her being was over, but, being over, gave way to memory.

She had been somewhere, somewhere very strange and

alien. She hadn't belonged there. Now the changes in her made that much obvious. She couldn't quite see how she hadn't seen it at the time.

Her mother came back. She, too, was damaged. She looked different. She was looking at Emma differently. Emma could see the change in her mother, but, like the strange and alien place, she could not quite see through to it. 'How are you feeling?' her mother said.

Emma had woken into another morning. Where this one stood in the order of things, she couldn't tell. The summer had disappeared overnight. Now this other morning dawned bringing another mother than the one she remembered from the last winter and spring.

'I don't know,' Emma said. 'I'm not sure. I think I'm okay.' Emma watched Violet Green arranging some new flowers. She watched the bitter concentration on Violet's face. This was the face of a person pained, as harmed and perhaps more damaged than Emma herself. 'What's wrong with me?' Emma said. 'Why can't I move?' The flower arranging halted, faltering for no more than a moment. But it was a moment heavy with significance. The air smelled of perfume and hospital and harm. 'Mum?' Emma said.

She observed her mother touch away a tear from the corner of her eye. Nothing more. The flower stems were being cut and thrust into vases. Cut and thrust. Cut. And thrust. Emma exhaled deeply. She closed her eyes. Somewhere, being kept at bay, a pyramid of pains were stacked against her. She knew of their existence, if not their actual location.

It all seemed to be this way, her whole life and body. All removed two or three or four steps from the neural centre. Emma's central nervous system seemed strung out beside her on the bed where she could see and slightly feel its quivering, its writhings. But the information it conveyed missed the brain, arriving perhaps at the next pillow to her own, waiting there to be picked up.

'Am I badly hurt, Mum?' she heard herself say. She herself said it, but without being entirely behind it. The answer, the outcome could not truly affect her. Not just yet, anyway.

Her mother stabbed home the last few cut flower stalks. There were two huge vases full of roses, red, white and yellow. The blooms seemed to glow, to shimmer with an inner light. A drunken wasp clicked and staggered at the bottom of one of the windows, kept alive by the false summer of the hospital heating.

Emma felt this way too. She too had a little light still on inside her. She too was being kept, the wintry autumn outside disallowed, since she had only that second leapt in from the late English summer sun.

'Mum?' she said again. Her mother turned one of the vases just slightly, the better to view her rose display. It looked wonderfully, brilliantly, sadly, sadly beautiful. 'Mum? Am I badly hurt?'

Her mother managed to look fully into her face. The look was self-contained, uncommitted. 'We don't know yet how badly hurt you are – Yes, you are hurt badly, we just don't know how badly.' The information came at Emma as it had left her mother, clinically cold. These were the facts as so far known. 'There's nothing to be done,' her mother went on, clinically conveying further information, 'not until you're better able to endure the tests. Nothing can be determined until then.'

Emma listened to the information coming at her. It all meant nothing at all. The important thing about it was the hardened heart of her mother. This, she could not recognise. So many changes, in so short a space of time. Barely the flicker of an eyelid and the world had turned, tilted, upending everything. It was like waking up in another place, parallel but absurd, like Alice in an altogether curiouser and far crueller Wonderland.

Emma looked at the roses. 'They're lovely,' she said. 'Look

at those colours.' Her mother looked at them, unaffected, as if the colour failed to reach her. 'Am I going to be all right?' Emma said.

Her mother looked at the roses, unaffected. 'Yes,' she said, 'you'll be all right.' The words didn't work. They fell flat, like dead petals.

'Mum?' Emma said. She waited for a response. 'Am I going to be all right?' she said, sorry for the silence.

But the silence reigned, on and on. It continued, on and on, until her mother, without turning, simply said, 'They don't know yet whether you'll be able to walk or not.'

The roses reverberated with light and beauty. The world, all individual worlds feasted upon the sight and sound of them, their silence that still said, and went on saying, 'They don't know yet whether you'll be able to walk. Or not.'

'**W**hat have I done?' Emma said to her father when she saw him next. He walked into her little room with more flowers in his arms. There were more flowers than could or should be contained in so small a space. But he brought flowers, as Emma could see, to be bringing something for her. It was the only positive act he could think to do.

Emma couldn't yet eat solids. She was still being fed by drip. Strange the way the stomach didn't rumble, despite having been empty for so long.

For how long? Emma couldn't quite face the expanses of lost time yet. She had a day right now, a minute, this very second to contend with. To think back or forward in the long term would undoubtedly gather recognition into this wonderfully flowered moment; if she wasn't careful, she would have to know with terrible certainty what had brought her to this and what the consequences would likely be.

But as soon as she saw him, her father turning up with his arms full of this second's flowers, she found herself asking of him, What had she done?

'Nothing,' he said, smiling. The flowers took up all of the chairs, tumbling on to the floor.

'Dad,' she said. The flowers had come to nothing, falling, as if cruelly cut from their past and future for this second alone. 'Dad, your new car,' Emma said.

He stumbled, as if he'd slipped or choked suddenly. 'You haven't done anything,' he said.

'But,' she said, 'your new car. What have I done?'

Her father gathered up the fallen blooms, laying them on the bed by Emma's side. It looked as if he was going to ignore the question, until he said, 'You haven't done anything. A car's nothing. Emma, it really is nothing. You're what counts – you are all that counts.' He was looking desperately into her face. He reached out, gently pushing her hair from her face. 'Nothing else,' he said.

Emma swallowed. Earlier that day, she had felt a tingling sensation in the soles of her feet. Apart from that, nothing. Nothing happened there. When she tried to move her toes, the blankets had not stirred. The attempt became an act of sheer will, tormenting the brain. Like trying to move a cup by telekinesis. The cups would not move. The blankets did not stir. 'I have to know,' she whispered to her father.

He was not strong. Not knowing seemed, to him, like a pretty blissful, desirable state. He stood wishing not to know himself, hoping that he was not going to need to be the one to ruin his daughter's blissfully painless ignorance. 'There's nothing to know,' he said. 'You almost hit a truck. You managed to swerve off the road. You hit a tree. That's it. Nothing more to know.'

Emma had no memory of it. All she could muster was a feeling of fascination for an oncoming, unavoidable horror. That her fate was inextricably linked to that inhuman force of crushing, crushing metal, she had no doubt. Her too-still, benumbed toes told her that much. But, she told herself, there was no such thing as fate, no such force driving a car into a tree on a busy bypass. The only fate, the force behind the crash of metal had been her, Emma Green careering wildly out of control and into danger.

Her father could not talk to her about any of it. He arranged the flowers, throwing out some of the older ones, replacing them with new, exactly as her mother had. But he, as Emma watched him, laid the old dying roses out with a dreadful, anguished pity that looked as if it was going to break his heart. Her mother had broken the stems of the dead flowers bitterly, angrily driving them for good into an old plastic carrier. Since that moment of her first waking, Emma hadn't seen her mother and father together.

He came in. She came in. Separately. Emma couldn't ask them why. She didn't seem to need to ask. Realisation fell into place, but the relative emotions still fluttered in the background like humming birds.

He came in, broken with pity and guilt.

She came in, blinded by the anger of humiliation.

Emma had to have regular injections to keep the pain at bay. Her parents appeared between the jabs.

Jab, he came in. Jab, she came in. Emma seemed to be anaesthetised against her own parents. Just as the pain found the energy to begin to approach her from one side or the other, jab, away. Her parents, one or the other, appeared. No pain involved.

Cocooned from the oyster of the world, Emma watched. The nurses, doctors, her mother, father. From there, she was able to ask her mother, 'Where's Nan?'

Her mother's humiliation hardened perceptibly. Her jaw tightened in a cruel, honest resolve. 'She's gone,' she said. Emma said nothing. Something came near to her, but fluttered away immediately in a confusion of flustered hummingbird's wings. 'She was an old woman,' Emma heard her mother saying. 'She was ill. For a long time. Cancer. She didn't want you to know,' she said, looking now at Emma. 'But I don't suppose it matters now,' she said. 'Not now she's gone.'

o o o

They left her bewildered, unable to decide on what to think. Emotions flew round her like anaesthetised pain, two stages removed from her body and her being. She knew they were there, but couldn't, just could not attach them.

Then she had another visitor. She hadn't expected him to come and see her here. Not him. Especially not him. He came in at a time she didn't usually expect to see anyone. The approximation of a pain was beginning to encroach when he appeared at the door of her room.

Emma didn't see him come in, but was suddenly aware of his presence. She found herself looking at him, into his eyes. He stood by the door with no flowers or gifts, nothing but himself as a stark, honest matter of fact. She looked into his eyes. Yes, they were beautiful, dark, large, intelligent. There was a soft understanding in them, an acceptance of weakness that was not pity. No, definitely not pity.

He was good looking. Italian features, olive skin. Not too tall, but with an upright stature, young and surprisingly fit. 'I won't ask how you are,' he said, his warm voice as suddenly and as unexpectedly in the room as he was.

'Hello,' Emma said, to Robbie Britto's father. 'You've come to see me,' she heard herself telling him. It didn't sound, under these circumstances, such a stupid thing to say.

'Yes,' he said, coming closer, 'I've come to see you.' He stood by her bed simply looking at her. It was as if coming to see her meant coming to stand by her bedside simply looking.

'I've been listening to Central Radio,' Emma told him. 'I listen quite a lot sometimes. I haven't heard Rob yet.'

'No,' he said, smiling. 'He doesn't get to do any broadcasts yet. They have to start at the bottom. Listen again in three or four years time.' Emma smiled. Or at least tried. Something about Robbie Britto's dad taking the trouble to come to the hospital to see her seemed to affect her. It caught in her throat as she tried to smile for him. She had to swallow to take another breath. A prickle of tears touched the lower lids of her eyes.

A pain approached, surprising Emma with its sudden proximity. The jab was nearly due, but not quite yet.

'Thank you for coming to see me,' Emma said. He waved her appreciation away, shaking his head. 'Did Rob ask you to come?' Emma said.

'No, but he knows I'm here. I wanted to see you. I have some things to say to you.' Emma looked quizzically at him. 'I hoped you were all right. I hear you're quite badly hurt.' Emma felt the hurt quite badly as he said it. Strange, how as he said things, they fell into place. 'I thought,' he said, 'that you'd probably have lots and lots of friends and family coming to see you. But then I saw your father making his way through all the reporters on the news –'

'Reporters?'

'Yes. Outside. They're all out there. Good story, you. They're being kept at bay because you're so badly hurt.' Again he had confirmed Emma's hurt for her. Again she felt the true terrible consequences. '*Heigh-Ho!* magazine', he went on, 'are especially keen. They even accosted me on the way in. Seems that they think that they have some kind of right of access – your father doesn't think so. Neither does your mother.'

'Neither do I,' Emma said.

He smiled again, briefly. 'I saw it all on the news on TV. It was seeing it like that that made me realise your friends couldn't be here for you.'

'No,' Emma said in agreement, 'I don't have any friends now.'

'Oh,' he said, 'I think you probably do. They just can't get to you.'

'You have though,' Emma said. 'You got through.'

'No,' he said, smiling again, 'that's not what I meant. I didn't mean they can't get through the pressmen. I meant they couldn't get through *you*.'

Emma stopped. She knew he was right. He said things quite as a matter of fact. As soon as he said them, that's what they were, a matter of fact. 'I don't know what happened to me,' Emma said.

He paused, thinking about what she'd said. 'I don't think you're talking about the car crash, are you?' he said.

191

'No,' Emma said. 'I'm talking about everything but. The car crash is easy to know about. It's everything else. I've been somewhere. I don't know where, now. It's like – it's like –' she was saying, looking for the words to tie down the emotions that were rushing at her. The tears were harder into her eyes, one making its way over her cheek to the corner of her mouth.

Mr Britto reached out and touched Emma's wrist. 'Rob didn't mean anything,' he said. 'He likes you. But he likes lots of girls. He just says things. He doesn't think.'

The tears fell freely from Emma's eyes. 'I don't know where I've been,' she said again. 'It's almost as if I can look back and see someone else doing all those things I did. As if it wasn't me at all, only then I didn't know it. I didn't know it,' she said, holding a hand to her mouth. She was staring into the distance, staring away into the recent past that led her to this very moment, with Mr Britto standing in sympathy by her bedside, with the pain at her side approaching, augmenting, becoming more violently insistent.

'Are you okay?' Mr Britto whispered to her. He could see she was in pain. He didn't know where the pain was coming from. He couldn't know. Emma didn't know herself.

'I'm sorry,' she said to Mr Britto, turning to look at him.

He smiled, softly, softly. 'You don't have to be,' he said. 'It's not your fault, really. People should be apologising to you. I'm apologising to you, on Rob's behalf. And my own. Lots of people should be doing the same.'

But Emma couldn't see it. She'd done this, to herself, to her parents. 'I've destroyed everything,' she said.

'No,' he said, 'no you haven't. Things have been damaged, that's all. You're damaged. Everything can be repaired.'

'My dad's car?'

'No, maybe not. But that doesn't matter, does it?'

'My dad then? My mum? They aren't staying together. They can't look at each other. I know, I've seen them.'

'Everything can be repaired,' Mr Britto said.

Now the nurse was coming in with the medications trolley. The intravenous feeder inserted into Emma's arm throbbed in anticipation. Numbness, glorious unfeeling was there for the taking. Emma was supposed to take it, unquestioningly. But suddenly she questioned it. She wanted to examine the pain she was in to see where it might lead. Mr Britto stood there insisting that everything could be repaired. Could it? Surely it depended upon the extent of the damage? The needle full of anaesthetics lied about the extent of the damage. It made too much feel all right. Emma didn't know, nobody knew if she was ever going to walk again. Her mother and father could no longer face each other. She had chased her friends, including her best friend, away. Her grandmother had died.

The time had come to question the extent of the damage. 'Could you come back?' Emma said to the nurse as she came in backwards through the door with her tray of medications. The nurse turned and looked.

Mr Britto shuffled. 'It's okay,' he said. 'I'll go. It's time I was –'

'Please don't,' Emma said. 'Nurse, could you give us a few more minutes, please?'

The nurse glanced at the watch pinned to her uniform. 'Just a few minutes then,' she said. 'No longer. You're already slightly overdue.' Emma knew that. She could feel the reality of it. It was hard and fast, matter of fact. The nurse left them.

'Shall I get Rob to come in and see you?' Mr Britto asked.

Emma shook her head. 'No, I don't think so. I just – think it's –'

'That's okay,' Mr Britto said, 'I understand. It's up to you. You don't have to see anybody you don't want to.

'It isn't that I don't want to –'

'I know,' he said. 'I know what it is.' Emma waited. He knew what it was. He said so. So far, everything he'd said made some kind of a reality for Emma, driving home the hard and fast matter of the facts of her life. He knew. Emma didn't. She waited to find out.

But he didn't tell her. He kissed her very gently on the side of her face, whispering goodbye.

Emma waited. She didn't know. Anything.

But he was gone.

She was in pain.

The anaesthetics failed. Emma willed them to stop working. All night she lay fatigued and in extreme discomfort. She saw herself at last. What she had been, what she had become. Where she now was.

Her grandmother was gone. Gone. Meaning she had died. Emma remembered her as she was with her before it had all started. She remembered the kind old lady with whom she'd had such a wonderful relationship, before the money troubles. Before the egomania. Before the insanity. When her grandmother was alive.

She'd died of cancer, having suffered for quite some time. The old lady hadn't wanted her only grandchild to know. Emma remembered her on the day of the lottery win, holding her by the wrist and trying to tell Eddie that she had done well.

Yes, Emma had done well. Very well indeed.

Now she cried. She lay all night in pain and discomfort, biting off great lumps of her innermost emotions. She ate her heart out all night, knowing that what she had done had contributed to every bad thing that had happened. She was the driving force behind it all. More than the money, because money couldn't do anything for itself, Emma had been the prime mover. She was responsible. It was all her fault. Even her Nan's death, Emma's fault.

By morning, her eyes had been wrung dry, her heart a cavernous opening disturbed by just the faintest beat of a bat's wing. Discomfort clenched her every controllable muscle, grinding its way into her teeth. Her hair failed miserably, falling wet and fetid. She blinked continuously, trying to revitalise the dried tear-ducts in her eyes. Her eyes were sore, tired. The ducts themselves were fatigued. Emma could sense the effort it would take to cry again. She didn't have the energy left.

The anaesthetic had failed, as miserably as Emma's hair. For a while she had refused it, but had eventually to succumb to the nurse's insistence. But nothing happened. Or if the pain altered at all, it merely shifted. All night the physical and mental anguish washed round her body. It was like having bleach in your veins. Several times she had felt like crying out: 'I've done this! Me! I have done all this!'

The morning came sooner than words. The winter dawn crept into the room cold and uncomforting. Something was going to have to be done.

Something was going to have to be done. The nurse appeared again as if by the turn of the clock. The medications were again pushed through the intravenous feeder into Emma's arm.

'You don't look too bright this morning, Emma,' the staff nurse said. 'Are you feeling all right?'

'Will I ever feel all right?' she said.

'Of course you will. If you want to.'

Emma questioned that, again and again. She could feel all right if she wanted to. Could she? Did she want to? Was it worth the effort? *Was it?* Somewhere along the line, somewhere, you had to make up your mind.

Eight

'**D**ear Helen', her father read. He looked up at his wife. She was sitting staring into some spot too far away to contact. Eddie looked at his daughter. Emma nodded to him to continue. He looked back down and read:

Dear Helen,
   It has taken me over three weeks to write this letter. I hope you can read it before you throw it away.

He glanced again at Violet. She maintained her gaze unbroken.

I know you will have heard what happened, so I won't bore you with any more mention of it. First of all, this was going to be a letter of apology, but in the end it's not. I am sorry, of course I am, but to apologise begs forgiveness, which I wouldn't dare do to you.
   I am changed by what has happened. The changes force us all to move on. There's no going back, no begging forgiveness.
   I'm sorry for what has happened, especially for the way I treated you, but I'm glad I've changed. Whether I'll learn to walk again or not is something I'll have to find out, but, believe it or not, it's not the worst thing I have to face.

Eddie glanced up, then looked back down. His breathing was not regular, his eyes blinking too frequently, his voice unsteady.

Believe it or not, he read on, that kind of a challenge feels as if it has something to look forward to in it. It feels like the excitement of the occasional tingle I've been getting in my toes. The pain and the hard work of it is something for me to deal with. I can use it to drive me forward, because that's the only way to go. Injury has shown me that.

When I first started writing this letter, I felt as if I wanted to go back. I was wrong. There is no going back, neither do I want that.

I am changed.

I have done a great many harms to a great many people. It is to those people, and I would include you in this Helen, that I need to commit my energy to. You, my mother and father and my grandmother. The fact that she's gone (you know, I'm sure) alters nothing. She deserves

Eddie faltered, then stopped. His head remained down. He was blinking into the open sheet of the handwritten letter. His voice had broken down. His hand went to his face.

Emma watched her mother looking at him. She had worked so hard to persuade them both to come here, together, like this. She waited until Violet stood up, reached out, and taking the letter from Eddie's hand read:

The fact that she's gone (you know, I'm sure) alters nothing. She deserves my best efforts. I want to learn to walk again, before I can run this time. To do this, I need to find out about myself. Just as my grandmother said.

I've learned a lot, Helen. I've learned how much there is to learn. That's all. But it's an awful lot.

I've got a lot to look forward to. I will see you back at school, I will see you at Uni., even though I'll probably be a year behind you. That doesn't matter.

I'm looking forward to seeing you again. I'd love to see you, soon, if you could find time to come and visit me. If not, I'll understand.

My parents and I have no home at the moment. We threw stones at it then threw it away. I'm hoping we can make a new

200

home in a real house with a proper garden and neighbours like your mum and dad. I'm hoping for that and many other things. The one thing I have in far more abundance than money now, is hope.

So, I'll say goodbye, hoping to see you, here, very soon.

Your friend,

Emma.

There was a huge silence. Violet didn't move. Neither did Eddie.

Emma looked at them both in turn. The room was set, as if frozen into this moment. The letter was finished. Emma had changed.

She looked in turn at her parents. 'Do you think she'll come?' she said. Still there was no movement. No movement. The silence was massive, like the pause before the applause at the end of a brilliant performance.

'Do you think she'll come?' Emma said once more. Her father's face appeared tentatively from the palm of his hand. He looked at Violet. She was lowering the letter, very slowly, her eyes left staring into vacant space.

'Dad?' Eddie glanced at Emma. He looked back at his wife. The letter in Violet's hand hung by her side.

'Dad?' Emma watched him stand. He stood, stepping across to Violet. Ever so gently, he took the letter from her hand.

'What do you think?' Eddie said, ever so gently, to Violet. She looked up into his face. Emma watched their eyes make contact. 'Do you think she'll come?' Eddie said.

Violet was looking into his eyes, he into hers. Emma watched them. She could hardly breathe. The answer was so, so very important. Emma couldn't breathe. She watched Violet's head shaking slightly. For a second, for one awful moment, Emma thought that her mother was going to refuse.

'Yes,' Violet said, finally. 'I think she'll come.'

John Brindley

Rhino Boy

Ryan is an ordinary boy with an ordinary life – until the day he grows a rhinoceros horn in the middle of his forehead.

And now Ryan the school bully knows how it feels to be jeered at and whispered about, he knows what it's like to be the focus of media frenzy. He knows what it does to the mother he sneers at, the sister he snipes at, the father he hardly ever sees. And all Ryan's anger, fear, shame and disillusionment explode.

'fizzes with the pain and rage of a wounded animal – in this case the school-bully son of a deserting dad . . . psychological horror at its best. Brindley's richly imaged writing fairly burns with violence.' *Times*

John Brindley

The Terrible Quin

Suddenly he moves. He grabs James . . . swings him round, throwing him over the edge . . .

'No!' Maria has screamed before she can even realise what has happened, or even that she has screamed.

Maria and James's father vanishes, without explanation. They want him back. They're desperate. But their search for him turns into a living nightmare. It's oppressive, relentless and nothing can prepare them for facing the Terrible Quin.

A gripping thriller guaranteed to have you on the edge of your seat.

John Brindley

Turning to Stone

Some things die, other things live. It's what happens.

'Please help me,' she's saying to him. Tom, please, help me. Please, please help me.'

She hasn't slept. Anybody could see. She's been up, eating, being sick, making herself sick, eating again. Being sick again.

Now here she is, half killed by herself, by the madness that's got into her somehow.

This is the story of Tom, his big sister, Jazz, and someone else, who lives alone in a world of her own making. But she is the only person who can instill in them both the will to survive. It's about the weak and the strong, perception and reality. Powerfully told, compulsive reading – this is one book that you won't put down until you've read it cover to cover.